Finding Your *Forever*

BESS McBRIDE

Books by Bess McBride

Time Travel Romance

The Earl Finds a Bride
(Book One of the Fairy Tales Across Time series)

The Viscount Finds Love
(Book Two of the Fairy Tales Across Time series)

The Baron Finds Happiness
(Book Three of the Fairy Tales Across Time series)

A Ship Through Time

The Highlander's Stronghold
(Book One of the Searching for a Highlander series)

The Highlander's Keep
(Book Two of the Searching for a Highlander series)

The Highlander's Home
(Book Three of the Searching for a Highlander series)

My Laird's Castle
(Book One of the My Laird's Castle series)

My Laird's Love
(Book Two of the My Laird's Castle series)

My Laird's Heart
(Book Three of the My Laird's Castle series)

Caving in to You
(Book One of the Love in the Old West series)

A Home in Your Heart
(Book Two of the Love in the Old West series)

Forever Beside You in Time

Moonlight Wishes in Time
(Book One of the Moonlight Wishes in Time series)

Under an English Moon
(Book Two of the Moonlight Wishes in Time series)

Following You Through Time
(Book Three of the Moonlight Wishes in Time series)

A Train Through Time
(Book One of the Train Through Time series)

Together Forever in Time
(Book Two of the Train Through Time series)

A Smile in Time
(Book Three of the Train Through Time series)

Finding You in Time
(Book Four of the Train Through Time series)

A Fall in Time
(Book Five of the Train Through Time series)

A Summer in Time
(Book Six of the Train Through Time series)

Train Through Time Series Boxed Set
(Books 1-3)

Across the Winds of Time

A Wedding Across the Winds of Time
(Novella)

Love of My Heart

Historical Romance

Anna and the Conductor

The Earl's Beloved Match
(Novella)

The Dishonest Duke

Short Cozy Mysteries by Minnie Crockwell

Will Travel for Trouble Series

Trouble at Happy Trails *(Book 1)*

Trouble at Sunny Lake *(Book 2)*

Trouble at Glacier *(Book 3)*

Trouble at Hungry Horse *(Book 4)*

Trouble at Snake and Clearwater *(Book 5)*

Trouble in Florence *(Book 6)*

Trouble in Tombstone Town *(Book 7)*

Trouble in Cochise Stronghold *(Book 8)*

Trouble in Orange Beach *(Book 9)*

Trouble at Pelican Penthouse *(Book 10)*

Trouble at Island Castle *(Book 11)*

Trouble at Yellowstone *(Book 12)*

Trouble at Devils Tower *(Book 13)*

Trouble in El Paso *(Book 14)*

Trouble in Diablo Canyon *(Book 15)*

Trouble in Santa Fe *(Book 16)*

Will Travel for Trouble Series *(Books 1-3)*

Will Travel for Trouble Series *(Books 4-6)*

Will Travel for Trouble Series *(Books 7-9)*

Will Travel for Trouble Series *(Books 10-12)*

Will Travel for Trouble Series *(Books 13-14)*

DEDICATION

To all us anxious sorts out there!
There is room for us.
If nothing else, we make calm people look good!

Dear Reader,

Thank you for purchasing *Finding Your Forever*. Third in a series of time travel romances called A Town Lost in Time, *Finding Your Forever* is set in mystical Washington State at the turn of the twentieth century. Here's a bit about the story.

Deep in the forests of Western Washington, near the majestic dormant volcano called Mount Rainier, lays a small town that exists only in history. Partially submerged by a lake and largely buried by mud, weeds, grass and trees, Kaskade is lost in time. Unable or unwilling to die its natural death, Kaskade comes to life over a hundred years into the future on the summer solstice, hoping to capture new life for the town.

Not everyone who is taken will stay in Kaskade. Most of them return to the future on the next summer solstice. Who will Kaskade take next? And will they stay?

Brother and sister Jefferson and Martha Lundrum have settled into life as a lifelong bachelor and spinster. Does Kaskade have other ideas for them?

For those of you wondering, this series is based on a real lake. I've changed the name to facilitate the use of literary license in this work of fiction.

Thank you for your support over the years, friends and readers. Because of your favorable comments, I continue to strive to write the best stories I can. More romances are on the way!

You know I always enjoy hearing from you, so please feel free to contact me at bessmcbride@gmail.com or through my website at http://www.bessmcbride.com.

Many of you know I also write a series of short cozy mysteries under the pen name of Minnie Crockwell. Feel free to stop by my website and learn more about the series.

Thanks for reading!

Bess

Chapter One

Josie Brookman climbed out of the passenger side of her date's Jeep and crossed the secluded road to join him as he photographed a quaint little lake partially obscured from the road by trees. She had planned on waiting in the vehicle for Will, but he seemed inclined to linger long after he had aimed his camera...and presumably taken enough shots.

"Cute," she said upon reaching his side with what she felt was endless patience. "So how many photo stops does this make this morning, Will? Are we planning on stopping for something to eat? Remember? You said something like 'Hey, how about a picnic?' when you called me this morning?"

Will looked down at her from his six-foot lanky frame and grinned with perfect teeth. Carefree chestnut hair curled around his ears, hugging the back of his neck. In a forest-green T-shirt, tan cargo shorts and hiking boots, he was the epitome of an outdoorsy guy. In fact, he was, and despite his handsome looks, Josie wasn't sure the librarian in her was very compatible with Mr. Nature himself.

"Hey, how about a picnic?" Will repeated in his warm baritone. "Right here?" He nodded toward the lake, chuckling in the lighthearted way that had originally attracted her to him.

Josie admired his cheerful personality, but she had begun to wonder if opposites didn't actually attract after all. She wanted to laugh and thought people who laughed easily seemed relaxed, but she couldn't stop worrying, organizing and planning long enough to chuckle about most things.

Josie glanced over her shoulder at the quiet highway before turning forward to study the thickly forested stretch of land between them and the lake.

"You mean down by the lake?" She scanned the edge of the road for a path leading into the woods. "I don't see any picnic benches. I don't even see a path down there. The woods look pretty thick. Do you think there are mosquitoes in there? What about ticks?" She looked down at her ankle-length blue jeans and athletic shoes. "I'm not sure my socks are thick enough to go traipsing into the wilderness. I would have dressed differently if I'd known we were going on a hike."

"Relax, Josie!" Will protested, his smile broadening. His short beard was just a shade darker than his hair. "It's just a picnic down by the lake, not the Lewis and Clark Expedition."

"I know, I know, but how do we get down there? Do you see a path?" The edge of the road fell away abruptly and descended into a tangle of bushes and trees. Was she supposed to crawl down on her hands and knees?

"Sure, right there!" Will said. "It looks like people have traveled down here before. I'd like to get a couple pictures of the lake from the water's edge."

Josie looked in the direction where Will pointed and saw what looked like nothing more than a narrow rut leading down into the woods.

"That?" Josie asked faintly. "Is that an animal trail? What kind of animals wander around out here?"

Will laughed. "You're such a city girl! I think that path is probably man-made. But I suspect deer would also use it to get down to the lake."

"Deer!" Josie exclaimed. "Oh! I've never seen a deer in real life. I want to see a deer!"

"Well, it's the middle of the day. I doubt any self-respecting deer is just going to wander up to us for a bite of our sandwich, but maybe we will. So what do you say? Do you want to head in there and see what we see?"

Josie's stomach rumbled. "We would have to carry the picnic basket down in there."

"What basket?" Will said with a grin. "I threw a couple of those store-bought premade sandwiches in my backpack...in honor of you. I normally just do a piece of fruit and some trail mix when I'm out hiking or photographing."

Josie looked up at Will. They were on their third date, and she had a feeling it would be their last.

"Store-bought?" she whispered. "How old are they?"

"You mean the sandwiches?" Will shrugged. "I don't know. I just bought them. How old could they be?"

"I mean...did you look at the prepared date or expiration date or anything?"

"Nah," he said. "I'm sure they're good. Let me go get my backpack from the Jeep. Be right back!"

Will crossed the road, and Josie turned to stare into the woods again. The sun warmed her head, a rare event in Western Washington, and she was reluctant to give up the sunshine to head into the darkened woods. She could see sunlight sparkling on the lake beyond, but getting to the water's edge meant slogging through the gloomy canopy. The longer she stared at the forest, the more forbidding it became.

"Ready?" Will asked, returning to her side with a well-worn olive-green backpack slung over one shoulder. He had stuffed his camera into a side pocket of the pack.

"Kind of," she said, hoping she sounded more positive than she felt. It wasn't Will's fault that she was an indoorsy gal. When she wasn't working in the library, her life involved reading, crafting, crocheting and painting. It was small wonder that she enjoyed the rare moment of sunshine that warmed her scalp since she rarely found entertainment outside of her cozy apartment.

A shy child, Josie's parents hadn't forced her to venture outside and play with neighbor children, nor had they sent her off to camp during the summer. It seemed likely she had been shy because she had been the only child of older parents who enjoyed nothing so much as solving crosswords or fitting jigsaw puzzles together. The threesome had enjoyed home life, and she missed them terribly, both having passed away within a year of each other when she was twenty-three.

For the two years following their deaths, Josie had struggled with debilitating loneliness, finally deciding recently to try some form of online dating. Her first several dates had been disastrous, the men wanting to enter into physical relationships almost immediately upon meeting. Will had been her third attempt, and she had liked him instantly. A consummate gentleman, he had never pressured her for anything intimate, but Josie had also come to realize that they had little in common. In contrast to the other dates, Josie wasn't even sure that Will was physically attracted to her. For her part, she thought he was handsome, but he didn't make her heart race—an oddity because most things made her heart race.

"Here, take my hand," Will said.

Josie slipped her hand into his big palm, and he helped her down the narrow path. They entered the forest, and Josie was surprised to find the trail widening, at times expanding into two tracks.

"Looks like folks have been riding quads in here," Will said. "I don't hear any noise right now, so that's good."

Josie nodded. She would have panicked if she'd had to dodge noisy vehicles. Will had released her hand as soon as the terrain leveled out.

"Which way?" she asked.

"We'll just follow the trail. I'm sure it leads around to the lake."

"It's kind of wet in here," Josie said, studying the mounds of dead leaves that formed a carpet on either side of the tracks.

"It doesn't seem to get a lot of sun," Will said, striding confidently in comparison to Josie's tentative steps.

"No kidding. I hope we can find somewhere dry to sit."

"Oh, I'm sure there will be a log or something to sit on."

"A log? Don't those have termites and bugs and things?"

Will paused and looked back at Josie, who lagged behind.

"Probably," he said. "Everything's got to live somewhere, right? I think this was an old timber town. Bound to find some old log near the lake."

"There was a town here?" Josie asked. She scanned the forest again. "In *these* woods? They're so thick!"

"Well, I doubt these trees were here then. In fact, since it was a timber town, I doubt there were a lot of trees anywhere. They've all grown up since then."

Josie tilted her head back to marvel at the height of some of the evergreens.

"How long ago was that?"

"A little over a hundred years ago, I think." Will paused. "Let's follow this trail. It looks a little less used."

"Less used," Josie echoed with a sigh. Will had said that like that was a good thing. She followed him down a narrow path that seemed unlikely to have accommodated a human with two feet.

"Yes, I think this is probably a deer trail," Will said. "That would definitely lead to the lake."

"Okay," she said, holding back yet another groan. At that point, she was just following the food in Will's backpack. The "great outdoors" had given her an appetite.

Thick brush reached out to snag at them occasionally, and Will batted it away. Josie suspected she had imbued the foliage with sentient purpose and intent, but the unkempt woods worried her. To think that a town had once existed here made the trek through the brush all the more unsettling.

Where had everyone gone? Where were the buildings? She started to ask Will, but thought better of it. She didn't want him to turn around, pause and hold forth on the subject. She just wanted to get out of the claustrophobic canopy of trees and reach the sunlight she could see filtering through ahead of them.

As if she had voiced her questions aloud though, Will did stop. He peered into the brush, and she followed his eyes. She saw nothing but bushes.

"What's this?" he asked as if talking to himself.

Josie answered anyway. "Nothing?" she offered. "So do you think we can picnic up ahead in that blip of sunshine?"

Will shrugged without turning away from his investigation. "Sure!" he said. "Let me just take a look in here before we move on."

With bare hands, Will parted what Josie thought could have been poisonous shrubs, and he moved into a thicket as high as his chest. She could still see his head but nothing else.

"Hey, Will, be careful!" she called out. She hung back, unwilling to touch anything more exotic than a tomato plant.

"Oh, wow! This is cool!" Will said, looking down at something.

"What is it?"

"The concrete foundation of some old building! I would have thought they would have bulldozed the old town."

Josie looked over her shoulder at the woods, now alive and whispering. What secrets were they hiding?

"I want to see!"

"Come in here."

"No, I don't think so," Josie said with regret. "I'm freaked out now as it is."

Will raised his head and looked at her.

"About what?"

"This whole overgrown woodsy thing. I feel like I'm in a fairy tale and some little girl in a red cape is going to traipse by on her way to grandma's house, followed by a wolf."

Will laughed, the sound far too cheerful for the gloominess of the area.

"That's funny," he said. He returned to his exploration, moving farther into the thicket.

"Okay, Will, so there's a concrete foundation. Can we go now?"

"Can you wait one more minute?" he asked. "I just want to see how big the building was. It keeps going."

He disappeared from view, and Josie's anxiety rose to a new level.

"Will!"

"Yes?" he called out in a muffled voice.

"Can you hurry it up? I'm actually getting cold. It's kind of dank and wet in here! Do I smell mold?"

Will's head popped up again. "That's just the outdoors, Josie. It is damp in here but nothing to worry about."

"Okay, well, I'm still getting cold. Have you seen enough?"

Will ducked his head back down for what Josie hoped was a final examination.

"Come on, Josie," he wheedled, his voice muffled again. "Come look at this! This concrete is probably over a hundred years old!"

"Really?" she asked. "Does it look different from modern concrete?"

"Probably! I don't know. Historical construction isn't my thing."

"Mine either, but I do like to eat!"

Will's head popped back into sight.

"Okay! I'll make you a deal. You come over here and look at this foundation, and then we'll go eat!"

"Will!" It was Josie's turn to wheedle. "How about we eat first?"

"If I were a gentleman, I would give in to you, but..." Will left the words hanging.

Josie's stomach growled loudly, startling her. She jumped and scanned the forest, as if the growl had come from a menacing bear.

"Okay, okay, one look and we're leaving!" she squeaked.

Will raised his head again. He moved toward her and parted the thicket to allow her to approach. Josie rotated and sidestepped in, careful to keep her hands high and free of the foliage.

"All right, what is it that you want me to see?" she asked, entering an open area that was heavily carpeted with leaves. A three-foot-high moss-covered concrete structure dominated the small clearing, resembling, as Will had said, the foundation of a building.

"You didn't tell me there was a clearing in here!"

"Isn't this great?" Will crouched to examine the base of the wall. He reached out to touch it but pulled back.

"What's wrong? Is the moss toxic? It's bright green. That's not mold, right?"

"No, no. I just got a strange feeling, that's all, like I shouldn't touch it."

"Then don't!" Josie urged. "Go with your gut!"

"Don't you wonder what kind of building this was, what it was used for?" Will asked in apparent fascination. "It seems kind of big for a house, don't you think?"

Josie studied the structure. "It does look big. I don't know. I don't know anything about historical architecture either." She moved over to Will's side, where he continued to kneel at the base of the foundation.

"And you think this is a hundred years old?" Josie asked. "The concrete looks in pretty good shape to me."

"Well, I think the town has been gone for a long time. Hey, can you get my camera out of my backpack? I want to take a few pictures."

Josie rolled her eyes but walked around behind him and pulled the camera from his pack. At the same moment, Will rose and wobbled. His backpack slid off, and Josie reached out to catch him as he thrust out an arm to brace himself against the foundation. She accidentally dropped the camera, and the forest closed in on her.

"Josie!" Will called out as if from a distance.

"Will!" she shrieked.

Chapter Two

"Miss. Miss. Can you wake up?"

Josie heard the sweet female voice before she saw the angel kneeling over her. She opened her eyes to see a stunning head of luminous platinum hair crowning a face notable for crystal-blue eyes and flawless porcelain skin. The woman wore her hair parted severely in the middle and pulled back at the nape of her neck. Her conservative high-necked blouse of pewter gray poplin only emphasized her beauty. Her gentle smile matched her voice.

Josie couldn't seem to make her mouth work to speak. She followed the woman's head as she turned to speak to a man kneeling at her side. Almost a clone of the woman, he sported a grin on his handsome face.

"Martha! Two of them? Is it possible?" he asked.

Josie had no idea what he was talking about, but she remembered she had been with Will. Something had happened, and she couldn't quite recall what.

"Where's Will?" she asked, pushing herself to an upright sitting position.

"Is that his name, Will?" the man asked.

His dove-gray suit jacket suited his coloring, but it was the well-starched collar of his white shirt that caught the eye. He wore it unusually high on his neck. Josie noted a pale-blue vest under his open jacket. Well-groomed platinum hair shone, with a side part and ending just at the collar. His blue eyes sparkled with what appeared to be humor.

Josie nodded dumbly. "Who are you?" she asked the couple. "Where's Will?"

"Will is lying behind you," the man said. "I think he is unconscious, but do not fear—I believe he will awaken soon, as you did."

Josie gasped and rotated on her hip to see Will behind her, sprawled on an unexpected bed of grass near the base of a concrete foundation. Her eyes traveled to the house that towered above them—a large two-story structure painted white. It lacked any particular curb appeal, seeming to be more practical than architecturally interesting. But it perched on top of a familiar concrete foundation.

Josie scrambled onto her knees to crawl to Will's side.

"Miss! Be careful. You've had a shock," the woman said. "My brother is right. Your Will should be fine soon."

Josie ignored the strange people in the strange environment, and she grasped the shoulders of the only thing that seemed familiar at that moment.

"Will, wake up! Will!"

Completely ignorant of medical knowledge, she bent down and listened to his chest. His heart beat loudly, and she straightened and grasped his shoulders again. She had no idea if he had broken his neck, was in a coma, slept, or was unconscious. She only knew she needed him to wake up and make the other people go away.

"Will! Wake up! I need you!"

"Poor thing," the woman murmured to her companion. "But two, Jefferson? I do not know what to think!"

Will's head lolled from side to side as Josie shook him. She looked over her shoulder at the angelic couple—both now standing on grass where there had been damp moss, next to a large house where there had been only an old concrete foundation. Josie barely noted that the woods seemed to have vanished, replaced by the house and other smaller structures as she desperately searched the area. A dirt road ran in front of them, bordered by other houses of different shapes.

Josie wanted to jump to her feet, but she wanted Will to wake up even more.

"Will! Wake up! Wake up!"

"Miss, I am certain he will come to," the man said, moving forward and bending down to place a restraining hand on Josie's frantically tugging arms. "I think it likely that he has simply fainted... or whatever it is that you people do."

Josie whirled around and almost toppled over onto her backside as she looked up at the man.

"*You people*? We people? Where am I?"

The woman moved forward as well and knelt down on the other side of Will.

"You are in Kaskade, miss. My name is Martha Lundrum, and this is my brother, Jefferson Lundrum. I know that you are frightened, but please believe that you are in good hands. We will not harm you."

Josie kept her hands on Will, as if they would drag him away.

"Kaskade? How did I get here? I don't even know where Kaskade is. Did someone bring me by ambulance? Where am I?"

Jefferson moved over to his sister's side and crouched down on his knees. He scanned the road, as if looking for someone.

"We need to get them inside," he murmured. "Too many eyes."

"I know," Martha said in a hushed voice. "But there are too many eyes inside the house as well."

"Are you talking about me? About us? I'm not going anywhere with anyone!" Josie snapped. She heard the rising hysteria in her voice, felt her breathing rapid and shallow. Her stomach twisted in knots.

"You don't understand!" Josie continued. "I don't do anxiety. That is, I do anxiety, but I don't *want* to do anxiety. I'm a naturally anxious person, so I'm stressed, and I don't want to be stressed, and I'm confused, and I don't know what is happening, and what is happening? Who are you? Where am I? What's wrong with Will?"

"Nothing, I don't think," Will said.

Josie gasped and turned to Will, whose brown eyes had opened. From the way his gaze darted around, Josie knew he was as stunned as she.

"Oh, Will!" she exclaimed thankfully. She grasped his shoulders and gave him a shake. "You scared me! I thought you were in some kind of coma. I don't know where we are or what's happened. I don't think I'm dreaming though. Or am I?"

Will pushed himself upright and looked at the people on his left.

"Hello," he said in an infuriatingly calm and pleasant tone. "Who are you?"

Martha's cheeks bloomed.

"I am Martha Lundrum, and this is my brother, Jefferson Lundrum. We own this boardinghouse."

Josie looked up at the house. A boardinghouse? Did Martha mean a bed and breakfast?

"Will Wright," he introduced himself. "What happened?" Will directed his question to the couple, a fact that irritated Josie.

The Lundrums exchanged a silent glance and then raised their eyes as if to survey the road once again.

"We would be happy to tell you, but we must get you inside before anyone sees you here, especially given the way you are dressed." Jefferson smiled conspiratorially, but Josie couldn't understand what he found so amusing. She dropped her eyes to her long-sleeved powder-blue cotton button-down shirt and blue jeans.

"What are you talking about?" she asked. "Get us inside? How we're dressed? What is going on?"

"Josie, let's just cooperate for now," Will said. "I'm sure we'll find out what Jefferson means eventually."

He pushed himself to a standing position. Martha and Jefferson rose as well, both tall, with Jefferson standing about the same height as Will. Josie stared up at the group from her position on the ground, noting that Will couldn't seem to keep his eyes off Martha's beautiful blushing face.

Jefferson reached out a hand to Josie. "Come inside, Josie. I promise that you are safe with us."

His charming smile should have reassured her. Maybe it did, but Josie wasn't about to relax for any reason.

She glanced at his strong-looking hand, and declining his touch, she pushed herself to her feet.

"I'll follow your lead, Will, but I'm not happy about this!" she muttered. "Don't you even want to know where we are?"

Will barely looked over his shoulder at Josie.

"We're in Kaskade," he said. "I can see the lake from here."

Josie followed his eyes. She saw nothing but the wood shingles of nearby houses.

"The view must be nice up there," she said. "I thought there was no town here anymore."

"So did I," Will murmured. "So did I."

"Will you come inside now?" Martha asked.

Will nodded, and Martha gathered up her skirts like some character out of an old Western movie and climbed the wooden stairs to the front door. Will followed, and Josie hesitated, looking over her shoulder to scan the area once more. From the top of the stairs, she did see a glimpse of the lake over the edge of rooftops. Jefferson waited behind her, as if to ensure that she didn't take off on a run—something she might have done if Will had agreed to escape with her.

Escape was the operative word as Josie followed Martha and Will up the stairs. She felt trapped, and she wanted out. She wanted to go home to her apartment and bury her head under the covers...or wake up from the nightmare. Either one would have been fine.

Josie reluctantly followed Will and Martha into the house. A foyer opened up to a hall, and a wooden staircase on the right led to the second floor. Dark-red carpet covered much of the hardwood floor in the foyer and hallway.

"Come down to the kitchen," Martha said. "I can shut the door there, and we can have some privacy."

Josie noticed that Will seemed ready to follow Martha docilely. She hesitated, unwilling to descend into the bowels of the large house, so to speak.

Jefferson put an encouraging hand on her elbow, and she shook him off.

"Don't push me!" she barked.

"Pardon me!" He stepped back, raising his hands as if to show he was harmless.

Nothing was harmless to Josie at that moment. She kept one eye on Jefferson while turning to Will.

"Will!" she whispered urgently. "We don't know what's going on here. Don't you want to ask questions before they 'shut doors' and 'have privacy'? What if this is some kind of asylum thingy or something? It has a prison kind of look to it!"

Josie ignored Martha's gasp, averting her eyes from the look of hurt on the woman's face.

"Josie! Stop that!" Will snapped in an unusual display of irritation. He looked over Josie's head toward Jefferson, then back at Martha. "Forgive her. She's an anxious kind of person."

"Will!" Josie protested. "That's not nice!"

Will turned to face her and put his hands on her shoulders. "I'm sorry, Josie. I'm not trying to be mean, but you're being kind of rude. Let's find out from Martha and Jefferson what's going on. I seriously doubt that they intend to hurt us. Can you get yourself under control for a bit?"

Josie's eyes widened. "Me? *I* need to get under control? You do see how surreal this whole thing is, right? Am I the only sane one around here?"

Will dropped his hands and shook his head.

"I doubt it," he said. He turned to Martha. "Can she wait here by the door while we talk in the kitchen?"

"What? No! Wait! I'm not staying here by myself. Forget it!" Josie spoke in breathless gasps. "I'm going with you."

"Okay then," Will replied calmly. "I guess we'll follow you after all," he said to Martha.

They followed Martha down the hall toward an open door that led to a vintage kitchen. A rectangular wooden farmhouse table dominated the center of the room. Covered in pots and pans, it probably served as both a kitchen island and dining table. Martha and Jefferson pulled out several chairs.

"Would you like some coffee?" she asked.

"I don't drink coffee, but thanks," Will said. "Do you have any water? I think I might be dehydrated."

Josie stared at the antique steel stove set against one wall, where an old-fashioned blue enamel coffee urn sat atop one of the slip plates. A basket of wood sat on the floor beside the stove.

"Yes, of course," Martha said. "Josie, would you like coffee?"

Josie didn't know what to say. She loved coffee, but she wasn't about to drink or eat anything until she better understood what was going on.

"No, thank you," she edged out.

"I would welcome a cup of coffee," Jefferson said, seating himself at the table.

Martha retrieved a plain glass tumbler and white ceramic cup from an open cabinet, setting them on the wooden counter. She opened up what look like a large oak cabinet and retrieved a glass water jug to fill the tumbler.

Josie leaned forward to study the cabinet. "Is that an old ice box?"

"Yes, it is," Martha said with a bright smile, "though we call them refrigerators now. It is kept cold with ice though. This one is quite new actually. I only bought it last year!"

She set the glass down in front of Will before returning to the stove to pour her brother a cup of coffee from the blue urn.

"I'm sorry. Did you say 'we call them refrigerators now'?" Josie repeated. "What does that mean? Why do you say now?"

She turned to Will, drinking his water. "Will, ask something!"

Will smiled placidly and shook his head. "I wouldn't know what to ask," he said with a shrug.

"No, you probably do not," Martha said, seating herself. "We have dallied long enough." She glanced at Jefferson, who nodded. "You have traveled through time to the year 1910."

CHAPTER THREE

Martha spoke slowly and clearly in the silence of the kitchen, and yet Josie thought she must have misunderstood.

"What?" she asked faintly. Her eyes darted from face to face. Martha's expression was sympathetic, Jefferson looked both amused and compassionate, and Will continued to watch Martha with fascination, as if he hadn't heard any strange words at all.

Martha smiled gently in Josie's direction. "You are in Kaskade during its heyday. It is the summer solstice, and you were brought back in time. As far as we know, you cannot travel back to your own time for a year until the next summer solstice."

"What on earth are you talking about?" Josie asked. She heard words, but they really weren't making any sense. She looked at Will.

"Say something, Will!"

Will stopped staring at Martha across the table long enough to turn in Josie's direction to his right.

"This is wild!" he said with a broad smile before returning his attention to the Lundrums.

"Wild?" Josie rasped. "Is that all you have to say?" She fought her instinct to get up and run out the door. She had no idea where she was and no idea how to get home. That Martha had said she was in a town called Kaskade and couldn't go home for about a year made no sense at all. None.

"No, actually, I do have questions," Will said, still grinning.

He addressed Martha and Jefferson. "So you say that we traveled through time? And the year is 1910?"

They nodded.

"What is this about the summer solstice? You're right. It is the summer solstice. I noticed that on the weather app this morning."

Martha nodded in Jefferson's direction, and Jefferson spoke, his cheerful expression hardly commensurate with the nightmarish situation in which Josie found herself. In fact, Josie noted that Jefferson and Will both sported the same sappy grins. Did both men share the same carefree personalities?

"Since the turn of the century, our little town of Kaskade has had a propensity for snatching up people from the future and transporting them to the past. To date, the town has only taken one person per year—nine before today—but it appears that Kaskade chose both of you...or one of you traveled to the past by mistake." Jefferson's crystal-blue eyes twinkled as he paused, as if to wait for questions.

"That would be me!" Josie sputtered. "*If* I believed a word you just said. Time travel! Come onnnnn!"

She eyed the puffed sleeves of Martha's blouse and the unusually high collar of Jefferson's shirt with growing dread. Unless she was sitting in a well-designed set on a stage in a theater, everything about her environment and the people in it seemed historical. She didn't know anything about the early nineteen hundreds, but the kitchen seemed authentic. The "antique" appliances looked fairly new.

"It is true, Josie," Martha said in her solicitous voice.

Josie would have been more likely to doubt the woman if she'd taken a more argumentative tone. Like Josie's.

"I believe you," Will said with a firm nod. "Why does the town 'snatch' people? Your term, not mine."

Jefferson shook his head. "We do not really know. The few of us who know about the time travelers speculate that it is Kaskade's way of trying to stay alive. We are fully aware that it disappears in the future, that it is nothing more than a few concrete foundations buried under dead leaves, overgrown foliage and a forest of trees in your time."

Josie stared at Jefferson. "*Your* time?" she repeated dubiously.

"Which is when?" Jefferson asked, that irritating smile playing on the corners of his lips.

Josie crossed her arms and gave Jefferson a derisive look. "Please! Like I'm going to play this game."

"2017," Will responded.

Josie eyed him darkly.

"So you all think that Kaskade is trying to stay alive by bringing people back through time?" Will continued. "How would that work?"

Jefferson's smile wavered, and Josie jumped on it.

"So you don't know?" she mocked.

"No, we think we know," Jefferson said. "I just did not care to say."

"What does that mean?" Josie challenged.

Jefferson's face took on color, and he turned to his sister, who also hesitated before responding.

"It is so soon to speak of those things," she prevaricated.

Will nodded, as if he was satisfied with her answer. Josie's heart hadn't stopped racing since she'd first awakened to find strangers looming over her, and the Lundrums' cryptic comments did nothing to ease her fears.

"When would be a good time?" Josie snapped.

Martha would not be riled.

"When you accept that you have traveled through time. I do not think you are yet at that place, Josie."

Josie drew in a sharp breath. She glanced at Will, who apparently was "at that place" Martha was describing.

"Are you just going with the flow, Will?" Josie muttered.

"Actually, yes, I am. You might be more pleasant if you did too, Josie."

"I'm *not* unpleasant, Will! I'm *scared*. I can't believe you aren't!"

Jefferson clicked his tongue, catching Josie's attention. He gave her a sympathetic look that held none of his usual amusement.

"We understand that you are frightened, Josie," Jefferson said. "Everyone who was dragged back through time has been equally terrified and disoriented. You will soon meet others who came from the twenty-first century, and I hope that you are reassured. Please bear with us. We want you to be happy while you are here. It is not forever. You can go home again, albeit in a year."

Despite her resistance, Josie found herself clinging to the candid compassion in Jefferson's eyes.

"A year," she murmured, pulling her gaze from his to scan the kitchen with its turn-of-the-century look. "I have a job." She almost whispered the last words.

"Yes, I am sorry," Jefferson said. "I imagine that both of you do."

Will shrugged. "I do, but it will be there when I get back."

"What is it that you do, Will?" Martha asked.

Josie thought it odd that they were talking about jobs as if they chatted over coffee under normal circumstances.

"I'm a fish and wildlife biologist for the National Park Service. I work at Mount Rainier."

Josie had known that information, but she hadn't shared Martha's reaction.

"Truly! How very exciting! You study fish and wildlife then?"

"I manage them, yes."

"That must be very rewarding work," Martha said. "How very adventurous!"

Josie eyed Will as his tanned cheeks bronzed. He rubbed his beard almost bashfully.

"What job will you have to leave, Josie?" Jefferson asked.

"Nothing as exciting as Will. I work at the library in Tacoma."

"A librarian!" Jefferson repeated. "Now, I find *that* exciting. I could bury my head in books for days."

Josie tried to hold back a smile, but Jefferson's complimentary enthusiasm touched her. Few people enthused about the excitement of the library.

"Me too," she said. In danger of outright ogling Jefferson's handsome face, she pulled her gaze from him and looked at Martha.

"What do we do now?" she asked in a small voice. "What have the others done, and when can we meet them? Are any of them women?"

Martha nodded. "All that have chosen to remain with us are women."

"Really? Why is that?" Josie asked, curiosity suppressing the remnants of disbelief.

Martha hesitated and looked at her brother.

"They married," Jefferson said quickly. "Now, we must think how best to house you. I presume you are not married to each other?"

"No!" Josie said hastily, glancing at Will.

"No," Will added in a more measured tone. "We were just dating."

Josie heard the past tense "were," but she didn't take offense. Will's trek through the underbrush had helped her decide that they had nothing in common. She had no doubt that he had agreed. The only thing she and Will shared at that moment was that they had traveled through time, and even then, their reactions had been vastly different.

"I hope that you did not leave family behind?" Martha asked. "Children? You said that you were dating, so I assume that you were not married to anyone else?"

Josie shook her head.

"No, I've never been married," Will offered. He grinned at Martha, who blushed.

Josie rolled her eyes. She caught Jefferson watching her with a speculative expression.

"I wonder if Kaskade made a mistake, Martha," he said in a musing tone. "Or perhaps it has simply changed its formula."

Josie narrowed her eyes. At Jefferson's words, she did take offense, but she wasn't quite sure why. Before she could protest what she didn't understand, Martha responded to him, her gaze flitting between Will and Josie.

"Yes, I do see what you mean, Jefferson. We will not concern ourselves with Kaskade's antics. For now, we must think of rooms. You will stay here in the boardinghouse with us, won't you? It will be a tight fit, but I think we can find the room for you."

"I'd love to," Will said with enthusiasm. "Thank you!"

"Thank you," Josie murmured. She still wondered about Kaskade, its "mistakes" and "antics," but didn't understand enough to ask any further questions just then.

"I do have one small room at the end of the hall that I could put you in, Josie. It is little more than a large closet where I store linens and was not intended as a bedroom, but it is all I have at the moment that is private enough for a lady. We can put a folding cot in there. People do tend to come and go, and I hope to have some rooms freed up within a week or two. Having said that, dear brother, I wonder if we could set a cot up in your room for Will, with the proviso that he get the first vacant room. I expect the Baker brothers to leave in a few weeks, as they have expressed that they are homesick and wish to return to Wisconsin."

Jefferson took the news of his roommate with good grace.

"That seems very practical, Martha. I thought I had heard that the Baker brothers were set on leaving. I will bring the folding cots down from the attic and help set them up when I return from work this evening."

"I can help with that," Will offered.

"Thank you, Will!" Martha said. "I would be most appreciative."

Josie remained mute and felt very ungrateful in her silence. She would help when the time came. She just didn't want to seem overly enthusiastic about it, like Will. She hoped with all her heart that she was in the middle of a dream, but it seemed more unlikely with each growing moment. If she had been in a dream, she certainly wouldn't have allowed the handsome Jefferson to rise from the table and announce that he had an appointment and had to leave for the office.

Of everyone in the room, Josie trusted Jefferson the most. Will seemed infatuated with Martha and hardly cared where he was. Martha seemed a bit secretive. Jefferson had been the most forthright, in Josie's opinion, and she didn't want him to disappear.

"You're leaving?" Josie couldn't help asking. "What about us? What are we supposed to do?"

Jefferson tilted his head and regarded Josie with a perplexed expression. "Martha will take care of you. She will answer any questions you have. I will make a detour to Dr. Cook's house and notify them that you and Will have arrived. No doubt they have been expecting someone, as it is the summer solstice."

"Wait! What? A doctor? I don't need a doctor!" Josie exclaimed.

Jefferson's typical amused expression reappeared. "No, of course not. Leigh Cook, the doctor's wife, came from the twenty-first century. She will be anxious to meet you. She can alleviate some of your fears."

"I'm not afraid," Josie mumbled under her breath, surprising even herself. Of course she was, but her go-to reaction since she had awakened appeared to be some kind of rebellion. She normally tended to be a more docile person. Hadn't she wandered into the woods with Will against her better judgment?

"I beg your pardon?" Jefferson asked.

"I didn't say anything."

Jefferson's grin broadened, but to Josie's dismay, he turned away.

"I will see you all this evening," he threw over his shoulder on the way out.

To Martha's credit, she too looked taken aback at Jefferson's departure. She stared at the two so-called time travelers with widened eyes.

"Leigh will come soon," she said, as if to reassure herself.

Josie took a deep breath and found an ounce of compassion.

"You know, I actually would like a cup of coffee while we wait for your friend."

Martha jumped up, as if happy for something to do. Josie had suspected the woman would be more comfortable doing something nurturing. She had that way about her.

"Good," Martha said. "Are you hungry? I have some cookies in the cupboard. Yes, let's have some. I know that I am hungry."

"Ohhhh," Will suddenly murmured. "Cookies! Is there any chance they're sugar-free? I don't eat refined sugar. Agave syrup is as sweet as it gets for me."

Martha turned, her cheeks bright red.

"Sugar-free?" she repeated. "No, I put two cups of sugar in the mix. They're sugar cookies. I do not think I have any of this agave syrup. What is that?"

"I *love* sugar cookies," Josie said, again surprising herself. She didn't care about cookies one way or the other, but Martha looked distressed in that way people who prided themselves on their cooking did. Josie's mother considered herself quite the baker, though her cakes and cookies, and in fact most of her food, had been truly awful. Josie and her father had done their best to work their way through all of her mother's cooking.

"I'd love to have some with my coffee," Josie continued.

Martha smiled widely.

"Good. What can I get you, Will?"

"A piece of fruit?"

"I have some strawberries. I was saving them for a pie, but I have spare. The garden is still producing."

"I don't want to put you out," Will said. "If you're saving them."

"No, no, that will be fine."

"Good! I'll help you pick more from your garden while I'm here," he said.

"Thank you." Martha said, lowering her eyes in a shy manner.

She poured out a cup of coffee and set the plain white cup and saucer in front of Josie, who thanked her. Josie and Will watched as Martha retrieved an old-fashioned round tin of cookies from a cupboard and placed some of the cookies on another white ceramic saucer. She set that on the table before reaching into the "refrigerator" and withdrawing a bowl of strawberries. Grabbing up some linen napkins, she set everything on the table before seating herself.

Josie had just bitten into the most delicious sugar cookie she thought she had ever tasted, when a soft tap on the kitchen door brought a beautiful auburn-haired woman into the kitchen. The woman slipped in furtively and closed the door behind her before turning and staring at the seated trio.

Martha jumped up. "Leigh! Thank goodness you are here! Meet Will Wright and Josie..." Martha turned to the newcomers. "I am so sorry, Josie. I do not even know your full name."

"Brookman," she said. "Josie Brookman."

"Oh! Look at you!" Leigh exclaimed. "Welcome! Welcome! I'm Leigh Cook, and I came from 2018. How about you?"

"2017," Will said, as if he was having the most natural conversation in the world.

"Nice!" Leigh said. Her startling robin's egg–blue eyes fell on Josie.

"You look shell-shocked, Josie. I know the feeling."

Josie heard Leigh say she was from the year 2018, but she looked every bit the part of an early-twentieth-century woman in a powder-blue ankle-length sateen flocked dress with a high lace collar, puffy long sleeves and a dark-blue belt at her tiny waist. A matching cobalt-blue hat topped her reddish-brown curls. She pulled out a hatpin and removed the hat before thrusting out her hand to Josie.

Josie dropped her cookie on the plate and accepted the handshake.

"And Will," Leigh said, extending her hand to him. "Two of you! Well, well, well, Martha!" Leigh said, giving Martha a pointed look.

Martha shook her head. "No, dear. Not this time."

"What's going on?" Josie asked, determined to break through Martha's veil of secrecy.

Chapter Four

Josie saw Leigh throw Martha a searching glance, and Martha shook her head in response.

"What did you mean 'not this time,' Martha?" Josie pressed, panic never really very far away. "There's something you're not telling us. It's frightening me. Is something bad going to happen?"

"No, no, Josie dear! Oh no!" Martha rushed to say. "No, there is nothing to be frightened of...more than has already happened to you. Leigh and I are making veiled references to the reason we believe Kaskade takes people from the future and brings them back in time. Frankly, this time it affects me...and Jefferson, and so I did not want to talk about it right now."

Leigh helped herself to a cup of coffee and sat down at the table.

"Sit down, Martha," she said. "I can do this."

"I am not at all certain the theory will hold up this time, Leigh," Martha said, continuing her cryptic comments. She resumed her seat. "I really think Kaskade had something else in mind...or as Jefferson suggested earlier, perhaps it simply made a mistake."

Josie remembered her earlier response to that comment, and she felt like repeating it. She held her tongue though, straining on the nebulous assumption that if she listened more closely, she could understand what they were talking about.

"Okay, even *I* think I need to know what you two are talking about," Will said. "Jefferson hinted at something weird about 'two' of us as well. So I'm guessing only one person has traveled back through time in the past years, right? And you think that one of us traveled by mistake? How would we know which one, and why?"

Leigh grimaced. "You're not going to like this, but you might as well hear it. We have a working theory that Kaskade brings people back in time to fall in love and marry someone from this time."

Josie gasped, and even Will muttered some sort of protest.

"I know! I know!" Leigh said. "That's certainly not what *I* wanted to hear when I first got here either. We think that Kaskade is trying to stay alive by bringing new life, but hey, we really don't know what Kaskade is doing."

Josie sputtered and swallowed hard.

Finally, Will asked a pertinent question. "What makes you think Kaskade brings people back...for that reason?"

Josie noted that Will avoided the word "marry." To date, he had been pretty tolerant of the nightmare in which they found themselves, but even he seemed to have reached the limits of his adventurous spirit. Josie welcomed him to the club of the unenthusiastic time travelers.

"Because in most cases, they end up at the house or business of the people with whom they fall in love," Leigh responded.

Will's tanned face blanched. Martha looked down into her coffee cup with bright cheeks. Josie quickly reaffirmed her assumption that she was the mistake and felt not at all caught up in the town's weird matchmaking schemes. Not at all.

"All nine?" Will asked. "You said nine people have come before us?"

"No, not all nine have remained. Some returned to the future. One man meant to come back, but for some reason didn't or couldn't. The ones who have stayed are Katherine, who married the minister who found her; Emily who married Luke...he found her. I wish you could meet Emily and Luke, but they're out of town for the summer. Then there is me, and I married Jeremiah, who found me."

"But that's not even half of the nine!" Will's voice was higher pitched than usual.

Josie understood the implications, but she wasn't about to vocalize them. Martha's blushing face said everything. Will had been chosen to marry Martha, and apparently Will understood that.

While he appeared pretty smitten with her, he didn't seem like he was interested in marriage. In three dates, she and Will had never discussed the matter.

"No, not quite, but there were other circumstances which might have worked out, except that the traveler wanted to go home." Leigh grimaced.

"I...I..." Will stammered.

Josie noticed he avoided looking at Martha.

"Please be kind," Leigh urged, glancing at Martha, whose eyes were wide and stark. "I wasn't very kind when I first heard that theory, and I regret my reactions."

"I'm not trying to be unkind. I'm just—" Will stopped short and turned to look at Josie. "Why aren't *you* saying anything? You certainly had a lot to say before."

Josie blinked at his acerbic tone. "I don't want to embarrass anyone," she said. "I don't know what to say. I think *I'm* probably the mistake. Kaskade probably meant to take you, and maybe when I reached out to help when you lost your balance, it grabbed me too?"

"Meant to take *me*?" he exclaimed. "Why not *you*?"

"Because I'm the one who didn't want to go traipsing into the wilds, Will! So, yes, *you*!"

Out of the periphery of her vision, Josie saw Leigh and Martha exchange startled glances. She turned to them.

"*I'm* the mistake," she affirmed. "Will touched the concrete. I didn't, sooooo..." She let the words—and implications—hang.

"Let's not worry about that now," Leigh said diplomatically. "You're here, and you can't return until the next summer solstice. It may not really matter why you're here."

An awkward silence fell on the kitchen.

"Jefferson and I thought Will and Josie might stay here at the boardinghouse," Martha said in a subdued voice. "We will put a cot in Jefferson's room for Will until I have a vacancy, and we will put another in a small closet at the end of the hall that is not used. It is not a bedroom, but it is all I have for a lady for the foreseeable future."

Leigh nodded. "If you don't have room for them, Martha, they are welcome to stay with us."

Martha drew in a quick breath and nodded. She looked at Josie, avoiding Will's eyes.

"Would you like that? Leigh's house is very fine. I think she has several spare rooms."

Josie swallowed hard. She had no idea what to do. She exchanged a glance with Will.

"You are no doubt finding it difficult to make a decision since you are probably still in shock," Martha said. She turned to Leigh. "I did not dare hope to ask—and it does seem so foolish since I run a boardinghouse—but might they stay with you? I thought I had hit upon a satisfactory plan, but if you have the spare rooms, that would be much more practical, would it not?"

"I don't know what to say," Josie finally uttered.

"I know," Leigh said with a sympathetic smile. "You'll be fine with us. My husband is a doctor, so that comes in handy on occasion, and I have a housekeeper who takes care of almost everything. If you don't mind stepping over a fourteen-month-old wannabe toddler, I would love to have both you and Will stay for as long as you need."

Josie looked to Martha, who nodded encouragingly.

"The room I was going to put you in really is a closet."

Josie glanced at Will who appeared uncomfortable. "Will? Should we take Leigh up on her offer?"

"I don't know what to do," he finally said. "I have no way to pay rent or anything right now. Neither one of us does. I left my wallet in the Jeep, but I didn't have much in it anyway."

"Twenty-first-century dollars wouldn't work here anyway," Leigh said. "And while we're on the subject, very few people know about the time traveling. We keep the secret closely guarded. People wouldn't understand any more than they would in our time." She paused. "Please don't worry about money for now. I did...we all did when we first arrived."

Josie swung her head to look at Martha.

"No, Leigh did not mean me," Martha said. "I was born in 1880." She smiled sweetly.

"We'll have to get both of you some other clothing," Leigh added. "The shorts will probably raise some eyebrows, Will. We'll have to get you a dress to wear as well, Josie." She turned to Martha. "Do you have some clothing they can borrow just to get back to my house? Maybe a pair of Jefferson's old trousers and a skirt? They can probably scoot along without too much notice in the shirts they're wearing."

"Are people going to be staring at us?" Josie asked, anxiety rising yet again. "What if they talk to us? Ask us questions? I don't know what to say. What should I say?"

"Everything will be all right, Josie," Martha said. "There is nothing to fear. Fortunately, you did not travel to the dark ages. All of our travelers have managed to live their lives without discovery."

"She's right, Josie," Leigh said. "I don't worry about it anymore. I can't share details of my former life, but what's the worst they could do if they discovered me?"

"Lock you up? Perform science experiments on you? You still don't have a lot of rights in 1910, do you?"

Leigh quirked a dark eyebrow and shook her head. "No, not really, especially as a woman. I have to admit that I shared the same fears as you are now. They've passed." She paused. "Okay, maybe they've *eased*. Maybe they'll always be there, but I hope you trust that we will protect you and Will."

Josie looked at Will, who nodded.

"I trust you," Josie said. "I hope that you can find it in your heart to put up with my anxieties. I tend to run on anxiety, so I'm probably not the best person to get caught up in a time traveling adventure. This might just be Will's kind of thing." She looked at Will. "I haven't known him long, but he seems very adventurous."

Will grinned, seeming to relax. Josie wondered if it was because they would be putting distance between themselves and the unmarried Lundrum siblings.

"So you are a couple?" Leigh asked directly. She shot another glance at Martha, and Josie understood why.

"No!" Will said quickly. He glanced at Josie. "I didn't mean it to sound like that, but we're just dating."

Josie decided to put him out of his misery. "We were actually on our last date, weren't we, Will?" She grinned to take the sting out of the words. "Will and I hadn't talked about it, but while we liked each other, we had very different interests and lifestyles. Is that fair to say, Will?"

Will's tanned cheeks bronzed above his beard. "Seems like a private conversation we should have had," he said, though he nodded agreement.

"Sorry," Josie murmured, chastened. She noted that both Leigh and Martha dropped their eyes to the table. An uncomfortable silence followed, finally broken by Leigh.

"I need to get back and relieve Mrs. Jackson from watching Jeri," Leigh said. "Did you have anything they could borrow, Martha?"

"Yes, of course," she said, rising. She scanned the kitchen. "I do not think I should take you upstairs, as I do have boarders who are here during the day. I will bring the clothing downstairs, and you can change in the pantry over there." She pointed to a closed door in the kitchen.

She left the room, and Leigh tilted her head as she regarded Will and Josie.

"I know you're overwhelmed. I was too when I came here two years ago. Well, when I was 'kidnapped,' to all intents and purposes. How can I help? Is there anything I can say to ease your minds or any questions you have?"

"I'm concerned about how to make a living," Josie said. "Any ideas?"

"You don't have to rush into anything, but I understand your concerns. What did you do in the twenty-first century?"

"I'm a librarian."

"And you, Will?"

"I'm a fish and wildlife biologist for the National Park Service. I work at Mount Rainier. Worked," he amended.

"Nice jobs!" Leigh said with a grin. "Kaskade doesn't have a library, but that doesn't mean they couldn't use one...or a bookstore. It's not as easy to get to Mount Rainier in 1910 as it is in the future, Will. I don't know anything about fish or wildlife, but someone around here will. I can't believe your skills won't come in handy here."

Will nodded. "I hope so. I'm sure I can rustle some sort of employment up while I'm here."

"I'm sure you will."

Martha returned, closing the door quietly behind her. She carried a handful of material and laid the garments out over the back of one of the kitchen chairs.

"I brought an entire suit of Jefferson's. He has plenty. I also brought a waist along with a skirt for Josie."

"A waist?" Josie repeated, rising to look at the clothing.

Will stood as well.

"A shirtwaist, a blouse," Leigh explained. "1910-style."

"Oh! Okay."

"I am afraid that I was not able to find any clean ladies' undergarments," Martha said with a blushing glance in Will's direction. "I have not done my laundry, and I had nothing suitably clean! Please forgive me."

"That's fine, Martha," Leigh said with a chuckle. "I'm sure Josie will thank you for that. Why don't you change first, Josie?" Leigh lifted a fluffy white blouse and black-and-white plaid serge skirt from the pile and handed them to Josie.

"I am afraid you will have to wear your own shoes, which I believe you call athletic shoes," Martha said, moving to open the door to the pantry. "My shoes would be much too large for you."

"That's fine," Josie said, happy to keep her own footwear. She stepped into the closet and eyed the wooden shelves lined with canned goods as well as pots, pans, dishes and linens. Several bins held potatoes and onions.

"There is no light in here, but if you leave the door open a bit, you'll be able to see," Martha said. "I promise you that no one will peek at you."

"Okay," Josie responded.

Martha pulled the door almost shut, and Josie set the garments down on a barrel of something or another. Although the pantry was dark, she could see well enough. She examined the blouse Martha had given her. Made of linen, it seemed to button down the front, thank goodness. She unbuttoned her shirt and set it aside on a shelf to slip into the blouse.

The shoulders of the long sleeves were enormously high, and try as she might, Josie could not flatten the stiff puffs. She felt ridiculous and a bit like a football linebacker but recalled that Leigh and Martha carried the style off well. The collar was high and stiff as well, and she struggled to button it. The front of the blouse puffed out with excessive material in the oddest fashion. Josie wondered if she was supposed to have the chest to fill it out. Martha was slender, but again the style of blouse looked well on her.

Josie looked down at her jeans. She saw no way to balance herself in the pantry to untie and remove her athletic shoes. No one would know if she wore her jeans. She picked up the skirt and stepped into the waist. Pulling it up over her hips, she buttoned it in the back and looked down to see the effect. The skirt spread out from her hips in an A-line shape and draped the floor. Josie recalled that Martha was about half a foot taller, and the skirt obviously reflected her height.

Josie sighed heavily, picked up her blouse, grabbed up the hem of Martha's skirt and stepped out of the pantry. Her cheeks burned as all three people in the kitchen turned to look at her. Leigh grinned widely, a spark of amusement in her eyes. Will stared at her as if she had emerged from a dark lagoon. Martha rushed forward to fuss over her.

"Oh dear! I was afraid the skirt would be too long. It will have to do until you reach Leigh's house. She is of a similar size to you and can loan you clothing that fits better. Let me do your hair."

To Josie's surprise, Martha pulled several hairpins from her own hair and expertly twisted Josie's shoulder length hair into a bun at her crown without need of a hairbrush.

"Your turn, Will," Leigh said while Martha secured pins into Josie's hair. Leigh picked up a jaunty chocolate-brown pinstriped suit and companion white shirt. Will eyed the garments with alarm when Leigh handed them to him.

Josie smirked at the dread on Will's face...finally. The women had found his Achilles' heel, the thing that took the smile off his face. Well, the second thing. Mention of marriage had been the first. Will apparently didn't like suits.

"Are those long sleeves?" he muttered, staring at the stiff shirt. "I don't really need to wear the jacket, do I?"

Leigh surveyed the clothing and nodded. "I think you should," she said. "Unless you're in work clothes, you would be expected to wear a jacket over the shirt. You'll be all right, Will. At least you don't have to wear a corset!"

Josie stopped grinning. "What? I don't have to wear a corset, do I? Why?" Her voice deteriorated into a whine.

"It is proper," Martha replied. She patted Josie's hair. "I have a plain sailor hat that I could spare. I will loan that to you."

"Thank you so much, Martha," Leigh said. "I'll be sure and get everything back to you." She turned to Will, still holding the loaned clothing. "Go ahead and change, Will."

He responded to the urging and stepped into the pantry. Josie sent the women a conspiratorial grin.

"He's really going to struggle in this clothing," she whispered. "I've never seen him in anything but a T-shirt and cargo shorts."

Martha smiled. "I must admit that I have never seen an adult man in short pants. They seem very comfortable. I noted that Will's feet were very large, and I did not think Jefferson's shoes would fit him, so he will have to wear those boots. They also look very comfortable."

Leigh chuckled. "They're hiking boots. They probably are comfortable, but every man in a fifty-mile radius will want to know where he got them."

"I did not care to say in front of Will, but he must comb his hair back," Martha said in a hushed voice. "I think it is quite lovely really, but the curls are quite wild. Jefferson has some pomade that he wears to keep his own curls under control."

Josie wondered about Jefferson's curls. She had seen that his hair was thick and well groomed. She should have suspected that he used product on it.

"I agree with you, Martha," Leigh said. "Why don't you go get the pomade and a comb? No, make that a brush. I doubt Will could get a comb through that hair."

Josie grinned again. It was true. Will's hair was a curly brown mop, and he was going to hate having to comb it back. Her own scalp was starting to hurt from the tight bun Martha had woven her hair into.

Martha left the kitchen, and Leigh turned to Josie.

"Okay, so quick, what's the deal with you and Will? I can't figure out if you're dating or not."

Josie shook her head. "*This* was our last date. He's an outdoorsy guy, and I am not. We met online, but we just don't mesh.

He's very relaxed about most things, and I'm kind of uptight. Why? Is that important?"

"Would it be a problem if he was attracted to someone else while you're here?"

Josie shook her head. "No. Do you mean Martha? I saw the sparks fly right away."

Leigh nodded. "Yes, I did mean Martha. You know why we think Kaskade brings people back through time."

Josie nodded again. "It's a bizarre theory, but if you believe it..." She let the words trail away.

Leigh looked as if she was about to respond, but hesitated.

"Remember, I'm the mistake," Josie said, heading off any other theories.

"I don't believe that for one minute," Leigh said firmly.

Chapter Five

Jefferson rushed through his workday, eager to get back to the house and help Martha with the newcomers. He had given the arrival of two time travelers to the boardinghouse much thought and had decided that Kaskade could have possibly erred on its latest selections.

Martha could not possibly find an earthy man such as Will attractive. She was far too fastidious and somber for such a match. And he, Jefferson? No. He had no intention of marrying. Twice now he had found himself somewhat enamored of women who had traveled through time—Leigh and Emily. After they had both chosen other men, he had reaffirmed his desire to remain a carefree bachelor—free of constraint, of emotional entanglement, of the excesses of women.

To be fair, he had not ardently pursued either Leigh or Emily, and he wished them both well. His own parents' marriage had been troubled, though he was not sure that Martha had ever known that. His mother had been an anxious woman, and his father a jovial sort who could not understand his wife's constant worries. Martha's calm temperament favored neither, but she had been the apple of their father's eye, and he the person she had loved most in the world.

To his great shame, Jefferson and Martha had avoided their mother as a matter of course. She'd fretted and muttered as she moved about the boardinghouse, often running boarders away with her constant nagging. It was Martha who had always managed the house with serenity that she had inherited from neither parent.

Josie reminded him of his mother, and he wished Josie well and vowed to protect her while she was his responsibility...for she was his responsibility. He did not deny that. She and Will had traveled through time and arrived at the boardinghouse. As tradition held, he and Martha should care for them. He hoped that Josie wanted to go home at the end of the year. He imagined Will would find nothing for which to stay, certainly not Martha. She was dedicated to the house and seemed to want for nothing else, including a husband and children. He could not imagine his sister finding interests away from the care of her boarders. They were her family, her children, though she had never referred to them as such.

Jefferson left his office just after one o'clock and hurried back to the boardinghouse. He stepped into the foyer, hung up his hat and listened for unusual sounds, but there were none. The kitchen door was open, and he strode toward it, expecting to hear Josie or Will.

Martha stood at the sink washing dishes, no doubt from the small luncheon she always prepared for several of the elderly boarders who remained in the house through lunch.

"Hello, dear. Where are our guests?"

Martha turned and wiped her hands on her apron. Her pale cheeks colored.

"They have gone to stay with Leigh and Jeremiah." Her crystal eyes sparkled, but not with joy. She did not smile, and in fact looked strained.

"Why?" he blurted out. "What happened?"

"Nothing," Martha said. She moved toward the kitchen table and uncharacteristically slumped down in a chair.

Jefferson pulled out a chair and joined her.

"We truly did not have the room, and when Leigh said that she had plenty of room, I could not keep them here."

Martha's eyes held what Jefferson imagined was moisture, but he couldn't be certain. She rarely cried.

"Martha, dear. Are you crying?"

She wiped at her eyes with the back of her hand. "No, of course not. It is the heat of the dishwater. I did so want them to stay though."

Jefferson covered her hand with his. "Oh, my dear. I am so very sorry. Is there no chance they might return when we have more room?

You said the Baker brothers might be leaving soon?"

"I think Will and Josie will be well and truly settled by then. You know Jeremiah's house has spare bedrooms. It is just that I miss Emily's company. Now that she has a baby, I do not see her as much as I once did when she worked with me here at the house. I did not realize how much I enjoyed having someone around during the day...other than the boarders. You know they do not care to climb the stairs, so they stay largely in their rooms."

Jefferson had not realized that Martha was lonely, but he heard the unfamiliar sadness in her voice. He patted her hand, at a loss for what to say. Silence fell upon them, and Jefferson chewed on his lower lip.

He too had looked forward to having the time travelers stay with them, and he struggled with his own feelings of disappointment. He thought he might have enjoyed having another young man stay at the house. The Baker brothers were of a different ilk, taciturn and not generally inclined to pleasant conversation. Jefferson had hoped to learn much about the future from Will.

He had assumed that Martha would care for Josie and that he himself would not be required to contend with her nervous disposition. He did think it a shame that such a beautiful young woman should be beset with such worries, but there it was. He wondered now if his mother had struggled with anxiety even as a young woman. For some reason, he had imagined that her behavior had come with age. Perhaps not.

Martha pulled her hand from his and rose to finish washing dishes.

"I wish there was something I could do to cheer you up, Martha," Jefferson said, rising as well. He felt at a loss, having dashed home to tend to the newcomers.

"You could do something for me," Martha said, her back to him.

"Anything, dear."

"You could escort me over to Leigh's house to see how Will and Josie have settled in."

Jefferson's reaction was immediate. "So soon? Did they not just leave?"

Martha turned around, her cheeks red and moist. She had said the moisture from the heat of the dishwater, but Jefferson had serious doubts about that.

"Several hours ago."

"But do you not have to prepare dinner?"

Martha pressed her lips together, an expression Jefferson almost never saw on her normally placid face.

"Surely this house can manage without me for a few minutes! We will not stay long. I only want to look in on them."

Jefferson blinked. "Of course, dear. Do you want to leave now?"

"Yes, thank you." She wiped her hands on her apron again, untied it, and hung it on a hook by the door.

Jefferson followed Martha to the front door, where he watched with interest as she peered into a small mirror on the wall while she positioned and repositioned her hat. Normally, she simply tossed the thing on her head and pinned it. He thought it best he remain silent when she pinched her cheeks and tugged on the skin at the corner of her eyes, as if smoothing out imaginary wrinkles. Martha's skin was flawless and translucent. She had no wrinkles. Still, she pressed her fingertips across the bridge of her nose, as if she straightened frown lines.

When she turned from the mirror, Jefferson leapt into action to open the front door. She passed through, and he followed her out. Martha walked purposefully down the street until they reached Lakefront Lane. She was uncharacteristically silent, as if lost in thought. Jefferson let her be, wondering if he really knew his sister at all.

Katherine Ludlow, the minister's wife, called to them from the porch of her modest two-story cottage on the corner of the lane. She set her broom against a wall, admonished her two small children to stay in the yard, and hurried to the gate.

"I know all about our new people!" she exclaimed. "In fact, I met them on their way to Leigh's house. Two! Two travelers!"

Martha smiled. "Isn't it wonderful?" she asked. "We rarely get gentlemen."

Jefferson gave his sister a sideways glance.

"I know!" Katherine said. "This is going to be a great year! They both seemed very friendly."

Such had not been Jefferson's opinion as far as Josie was concerned, but Katherine was herself a time traveler, and so perhaps

Josie had been more tranquil upon meeting her. Katherine was a warmhearted woman who had a reputation for being very successful at soothing and nurturing members of her husband's congregation.

"I am so glad," Martha said. "They were, of course, both quite distraught when they awakened near the boardinghouse, so I am pleased to hear that they have grown more comfortable with what has happened to them."

"I do not believe that Will was distraught," Jefferson noted. "He seemed very engaged in the adventure."

"Perhaps you are right," Martha said. She turned back to Katherine. "At first Will did seem quite keen on the concept of time travel."

"Why do you say 'at first'?" Katherine asked.

"Did something occur after I left to upset him?" Jefferson asked.

Martha's cheeks reddened. "The theory regarding Kaskade's purposes in taking certain people from the future disturbed him. That and the need to wear long sleeves and a suit jacket."

"He did look as if he spent a lot of time out of doors," Katherine noted with a chuckle. "He pulled at the collar of his shirt several times when we talked. But what is this about the theory? Do you think that Josie and Will were brought back in time for—" Katherine stopped talking and stared at them.

Martha shook her head. "No, it is not possible. I am too busy to marry, and I do not think Jefferson and Josie would suit at all. Perhaps Will and Josie were brought back to meet other people here in Kaskade."

"Maybe," Katherine said.

Jefferson could not like the skepticism in her voice. "No, Josie and I would not suit at all," he concurred. "I do not intend to marry. It is not for everyone."

Katherine nodded, her own cheeks red. "No, of course not." She looked over her shoulder toward the children playing quietly in the yard.

"We should be on our way," Jefferson said. "We were just stopping by the Cook house to inquire as to their well-being, and then Martha must get back to the house in time to prepare dinner."

Martha looked up at him, and his pleasant smile faded. Her eyes sparkled, but not with moisture. In fact, Jefferson was not at all certain that she didn't have frown lines between her eyes after all.

"Yes, I must get back...as my brother says. It was good to see you, Katherine. The children look very well."

Katherine tilted her head, giving the siblings a quizzical look. "It was good to see you two as well."

They went on their way.

"Martha, is everything all right?" Jefferson asked. "I know this has been a bewildering day for all of us. We could not have foreseen that the new travelers would come to us. It was quite unexpected!"

"I am perfectly fine, Jefferson," she said. "It is the summer solstice. We expected someone to come to Kaskade."

"Yes, of course, but to arrive at our doorstep? Astounding."

"I do not see why it should be so surprising to you."

"Well, the theory that is often mentioned. I am not wrong about that, am I, Martha? That particular premise will not hold up with us."

"The premise that the person chosen by Kaskade to travel back in time is destined to marry the person who finds them?" Martha sighed. "No, of course not, Jefferson. That would not apply to us. And here we are!"

They had reached the Cook house and passed through the gate to walk up to the front door. Jefferson knocked, and they waited for a few moments until Jeremiah opened the door. Expecting the housekeeper, Mrs. Jackson, Jefferson was surprised.

"Hello!" Jeremiah said, stepping back to allow them entry. "Hello, Martha! You look well, Jefferson. The house is in a bit of an uproar with our new guests."

Jefferson caught the droop of Martha's smile, but there was little he could say.

"Good day, Jeremiah," he said. "Martha did want to host the new arrivals, but we were short on comfortable living space. She told me that she was appreciative of Leigh's offer to host them."

"Indeed," Jeremiah said. "Two of them!"

It seemed that everyone had the same refrain.

"Yes," Jefferson murmured. They stepped into the foyer, and Jefferson laid his hat down on a table. He scanned the hall in search of Will and Josie.

"Will and Josie are in the parlor. I welcome your help in entertaining the travelers. Mrs. Jackson is upstairs seeing to rooms, and Leigh is tending to the baby."

Martha's smile returned, and she glided into the parlor just to the right of the entrance. Jefferson followed Jeremiah into the room. Will and Josie sat on a sofa. Jefferson always admired the room, elegantly furnished in forest-green tones, including the sofa, oriental carpet, and wallpaper. In contrast, the boardinghouse was Spartan, but then his parents never had the wherewithal that Jeremiah's grandfather and father had in their day. Though Jefferson knew Jeremiah to be generous with his time—including free medical visits for the poor— his practice was lucrative.

Jefferson blinked when he saw Will and Josie. Will's hair, only hours before so carefree and wild, had been tamed with pomade and combed back in a severe fashion, eschewing even a part. He looked unnatural and miserable in the high collar of a shirt that Jefferson recognized as his own, pulling at the top button as if it choked him. Will had pushed the sleeves of Jefferson's old brown suit to his elbows in a rather cavalier fashion.

However, it was Josie who held Jefferson's attention. A petite thing, she seemed lost in what he assumed was Martha's clothing. The shirtwaist puffed in every direction possible, and the sleeves had been folded back at the wrist. The skirt draped in front of her feet like a curtain too long for the window. The tawny hair pulled away from her face and piled high on her head allowed a better view of her high cheekbones and peach-colored skin. Dark eyebrows framed a piquant face that seemed particularly apprehensive at the moment as they eyed him. She adjusted the folds of her skirt, as if that could possibly make any difference in its resemblance to voluminous drapes.

"Is everything all right?" He spoke hurriedly, Josie's anxious expression troubling him.

"Yes," she said, belying her wavering lips.

Both Will and Josie had a glass of lemonade near them on side tables.

"Would you care for something to drink? Lemonade?" Jeremiah asked. "Please sit."

"Yes, thank you," Martha said. "Jefferson and I just wanted to look in on Will and Josie to see how they were settling. I do so appreciate you and Leigh taking them in."

Martha sat down in a chair across from the sofa, and Jefferson took another.

"Not at all," Jeremiah said, pouring lemonade from a crystal jug on a tray in front of the sofa. "We are most happy to host them." He handed Martha and Jefferson a glass tumbler each and seated himself on another chair.

"If you all don't mind, I think I'll take this jacket off," Will said, preparing to shrug out of the coat. He hesitated. "Is that okay?" He directed his question to anyone who would answer.

"Yes, of course," Jefferson said with a grin.

"I appreciate the loan though," Will said with a responding smile of relief. He went further and unbuttoned the top of the collar.

Jefferson hoped Will would stop divesting himself of clothing sooner rather than later.

Josie looked equally as miserable, and Jefferson wondered what he and Martha could do to assist them. He too realized they would be much better off at Jeremiah's house given the lack of suitable vacancies at the boardinghouse. What ailed Josie? He did not think he could ask in front of Jeremiah.

Jefferson looked toward Martha, hoping to capture her eye. She chatted with Jeremiah, Will and a silent Josie. Had his sister met his pointed gaze though, Jefferson did not think he could communicate with her silently. He had wanted her to take charge of Josie, to render assistance if need be. Josie's expression grew more haunted, and perspiration shone on her face. Jefferson could no longer hold back.

"Josie, is something wrong?" Jefferson asked. "Your cheeks are very red."

"I have to go to the bathroom! It's an emergency!" She jumped up and turned to Jeremiah. "Do you have one in the house, or do I have to go outside?"

CHAPTER SIX

All eyes focused on Josie, making her stomach ache even worse. Her stomach never did well with stress, and she'd been under a lot of stress that day. She had breathed deeply, she had tried to relax, she had hoped the lemonade would calm things down, but nothing helped. She had to go to the bathroom immediately.

Jeremiah rose quickly. "Of course. We have a bathroom inside the house," he said. "Just up the stairs at the end of the hall. Will you be all right?"

Josie grabbed up her skirts, forgetting that she still wore her jeans. Out of the corner of her eye, she saw Jefferson look at them, the corner of his lips lifting. But another look at her face erased his smile. Jeremiah accompanied her to the door and pointed out the stairs as she scurried away, her skirts hitched up to her knees.

Her stomach rumbled painfully as she climbed the stairs. She hoped that "bathroom" didn't mean some sort of chamber pot. She just didn't think she could handle that. Cold and clammy, she reached the second floor and stared down the longest hallway she thought she'd ever seen. A dark-red carpet ran the length of the hall, ending in an open door, beyond which she hoped was the bathroom.

She fled down the hall, ignoring several open doorways to her right. No time to find Leigh. She had to run.

Josie burst into the bathroom, thankful beyond words to find an upright genuine, honest-to-goodness porcelain toilet. Prepared to throw herself on the thing, she panicked when she realized how much material she had to contend with, given both the skirt and her jeans. With shaking hands and a wrenching pain in her lower abdomen, she unbuttoned the skirt, jumped out of it, unzipped her jeans and dropped onto the toilet.

Fifteen minutes later, Josie's troubles had subsided, and she pulled on a chain attached to a tank above the toilet. During her time in the bathroom, she had studied the white porcelain pedestal sink and claw-foot tub, wishing she could jump into the latter. She zipped up her jeans and washed her hands with a bar of lovely rose-scented soap. The towels weren't terry cloth but were white linen, and she dried her hands on the soft material before turning to eye her skirt on the floor.

The skirt reminded her that she would have to return downstairs and face all the eyes that saw her run upstairs. She was concerned that Jeremiah, the doctor, would want to ask her about her condition—something that had been diagnosed years before due to anxiety—but she was more concerned about what Jefferson thought.

Oddly, even given Will's robust health and outdoorsy athletic physique, she thought he would understand more than the others. Irritable bowel syndrome was a common complaint in the twenty-first century. She didn't know its historic origins. She didn't take medication for it, as it only occurred during periods of extreme stress.

She sighed and stepped back into the skirt to button it at the waist. She opened the door to find Leigh and an elderly woman chatting in the hallway.

Leigh hurried up to her. "Are you all right?" she asked, reaching to touch Josie's shoulder. "I'm so sorry. We should have shown you the bathroom right away. Believe me, Josie. I know what it's like to be thrown into the past. I should have remembered you would worry about hygienic needs. I know I did!"

Josie's cheeks flamed, in contrast to her cold sweat from earlier. Clearly, Leigh knew that her visit to the bathroom had been an emergency. Josie felt like her body would never calm down. Over Leigh's shoulder, she eyed the older woman—a plump gray-haired woman in a gray gingham dress under a large white apron. She guessed that was the housekeeper.

Leigh turned. "This is Mrs. Jackson, our housekeeper, cook, all-around woman who does *everything*! Mrs. Jackson, this is Josie Brookman, our newest lady traveler."

Mrs. Jackson nodded with a warm smile. Josie felt instantly connected to the woman. Her own mother had been a small but chubby thing.

"Welcome, Miss Brookman," the housekeeper said.

"Josie, please. It's lovely to meet you. I...I..." Josie instinctively wanted to say that she had kept the bathroom clean, but decided that would be odd. She already struggled with feeling out of place in the twenty-first century. Since she truly was out of place in the twentieth century, she thought she ought to suppress random comments.

"It is so nice to meet you as well," Mrs. Jackson said. "Can I make you a cup of oolong or pekoe tea? Would that soothe you?"

Josie winced. Even the housekeeper seemed to know that Josie had fled from the parlor with abdominal distress.

"No, I'm fine now, thank you, Mrs. Jackson," Josie said. "It's just something that happens when I'm stressed. Not always, but sometimes. I'm so embarrassed. Everyone in the parlor watched me run."

"Aww, Josie, don't be," Leigh murmured, eyeing her sympathetically. "I went down to the parlor after I put Jeri down for her nap, but you weren't there, so I asked where you were. It's not like they were sitting around talking about you...or your departure anyway. Besides, you can't help it. I'll bet everyone in that room has run for the bathroom a time or two themselves. I know I have!"

"Your room is ready when you are, Josie," Mrs. Jackson said. "It might do you good to have a lay down when your guests leave."

"I am tired," Josie said. "That sounds nice."

Leigh linked her hand in Josie's arm. "Well, let's go visit, and then you can come back up here and rest. Unless you're really wiped out? I can tell Martha and Jefferson that you've gone to lay down."

"No, I should go back down. I'm fine now."

Josie didn't know when she would see Jefferson...or Martha again, and she wanted to see them before they left.

"Good." Leigh led her down the stairs, chatting about clothing as they moved.

Mrs. Jackson vanished into one of the open doorways on the second floor, which appeared to be a bedroom.

"Thank goodness you and I are the same height," Leigh said. "I'll loan you some clothing. Martha is a tall woman. Her clothes are just swallowing you up. How tall are you anyway?"

"Five feet," Josie said.

"Me too!" Leigh chuckled. "That will make it easier to find stuff that fits you."

"I appreciate all that you're doing for me."

They neared the bottom of the stairs, and Leigh stopped and turned to Josie. She lowered her voice. "We're all in this together. Though I chose to stay, I'm still a twenty-first-century gal, and that's not something I'm likely to forget. We take care of one another, and that includes the small number of people from Kaskade who know about us and love us."

Leigh smiled and led Josie back toward the parlor. Upon entering, Jeremiah and Jefferson stood, their eyes on Josie. She could have died. Josie returned to the sofa, and Leigh sat beside her. Jefferson opened his mouth to speak, and Josie dropped her eyes to the green carpet with the thought that there was nothing anyone could say in front of the group that would not embarrass her. Nothing.

"Martha and I must leave," Jefferson said, rising. "We are so pleased to have you with us here in Kaskade, Will and Josie."

Josie's heart dropped. No! He was leaving? Already?

"So soon?" Leigh asked. "I just managed to get down here!"

"Yes, we have to get back to the house," Jefferson said. "Martha needs to start dinner."

Martha stood abruptly, an unusual speed for her given that Josie had only seen her glide with elegance.

"Yes, dinner," Martha said, her tone just as brusque as her movement. "It cannot make itself."

Josie caught Jeremiah's look of surprise as he glanced at Martha, confirming her guess that Martha's terse response was unlike her.

"Thank you for the lemonade," Martha said to Jeremiah and Leigh. She turned to Will. "I am so glad to see you and Josie comfortable. This was a much better situation for you. I could not have even offered you lemonade tonight, as I have no lemons!"

Martha tried to smile, but her beautiful lips faltered. Josie's heart went out to her, and she wasn't certain why, only that Martha appeared vulnerable at that moment, as if she was hurt.

"Oh, Martha," Leigh murmured, as if she too felt Martha's sadness.

Josie stood and moved toward Martha, who had turned away to join Jefferson at the doorway. Jeremiah, Leigh and Will stood as well.

Josie took Martha's hand and leaned in, as if to kiss her cheek.

"We would have been happy to stay with you," Josie whispered against Martha's heated cheeks.

Martha pulled her face away and stared at Josie with sparkling eyes. "This is better for you," she said in a hushed voice. "I cannot imagine what has gotten into me! This is better for you. There is so much more room here." She turned toward the door.

"Good evening," Jefferson said in a gruff voice, nodding in Josie's direction before saying farewell to the rest of the people in the room.

Josie wondered if he was aware of Martha's feelings, or even understood them. Martha sounded as if she felt rejected, and Josie recalled the discussion about changing houses. She didn't think she had been the one to suggest the idea.

When Jeremiah and Leigh escorted Jefferson and Martha to the front door, Josie turned to Will.

"You look miserable in that outfit," she said with a commiserating half smile.

"I am," Will said. "I've got to figure something else out. You can't tell me everyone here wears a suit and tie." He ran a finger around the high collar again.

"I shouldn't think so," Josie said. "Wait! Don't they wear shirts and suspenders and stuff? I'm trying to remember some of the older photos I've seen of anything in the early twentieth century. You said this was a timber mill town."

Will nodded. "Suspenders sounds good," he said. "Anything but this collar and jacket. And my boots! They'll take those over my dead body."

Josie lifted the hem of her skirt to display her athletic shoes.

"How long do you think I can keep mine?"

"Well, they're pretty well hidden by that skirt, don't you think? Do you like wearing all that material? It suits you, by the way."

Josie blushed, and then she blinked. "Hah! I thought you were serious for a moment! Very funny!"

"No, I was serious, Josie," Will said. "I'm not mocking you."

"Oh! Well, thank you." She was surprised by his compliment. She turned as Jeremiah and Leigh entered the parlor.

"I think I might have stepped on Martha's toes," Leigh said with a sigh. "I thought when I offered to host you two that she would be relieved. She gave the impression she would have to stuff you two into rooms and closets basically, so I thought she might appreciate the offer to have you stay with us. When she agreed, I thought she was pleased with the plan. Now, I think my impression was wrong."

Josie looked at Will, then to Leigh. "I can go back to the boardinghouse," Josie said. "I don't mind."

Will nodded. "I don't mind either. Whatever you think is best. I'm just grateful anyone is willing to put us up."

Jeremiah spoke. "I understand that Martha may have wanted you to stay at the boardinghouse, but in truth, it did not sound as if she had suitable vacancies. Now that you are here where we do have a spare room for each of you, I think you should stay. I do not believe that Martha would wish you to be uncomfortable if it is not necessary."

Josie and Will glanced at each other. Will looked as if he wanted to speak, but hesitated.

"What is it, Will?" Josie asked.

"It's actually a completely different subject," he said.

Josie waited.

"I guess I wanted to ask more about this *theory* everyone keeps talking about."

Jeremiah looked at Leigh with a quirked eyebrow.

"Kaskade's reason for bringing people back," she clarified.

Jeremiah nodded and returned his attention to Will.

"I wanted to hear your opinion," Will said. "Do you really believe that Kaskade brings people back in time to try to marry them off to inhabitants?"

"I might word it a bit more generously since I have benefited from Kaskade's peculiarity, but yes, I do believe that is the impetus for the time travel."

Josie felt as unhappy as Will looked at Jeremiah's measured response. That the doctor was unemotional about it made the answer all too stark.

"I see," Will said quietly. "People are saying that whoever finds us here in Kaskade is whom we're supposed to marry."

Jeremiah hesitated. "Those who found love remained to marry, with one exception."

"Do you mean Tanya?" Leigh asked.

Josie heard something edgy in her voice.

Jeremiah turned to her, a wide smile spreading across his face. His love for Leigh was apparent in the softening of his eyes.

"No, my love. I meant Matthew Wayne. You have heard us speak of him many times."

"Oh! Matthew!" Leigh's cheeks bloomed, and she stepped closer to her husband, taking his hand in hers.

Jeremiah turned back to Will and Josie. "Like you, Matthew Wayne came from the future. He fell in love with a young lady, but he had to return to his time to see to his ailing mother. He had every intention of returning to marry his sweetheart, but we never saw him again, and somebody else came the following year."

Will nodded. "So you think because Josie and I ended up at the boardinghouse that we're intended for Martha and Jefferson?"

Josie drew in a sharp breath and spoke quickly. "We already talked about this today. I think *I* was a mistake. You've only had one person travel back in time, and since there are two of us, someone guessed Kaskade might have made a mistake. That would be me. *I* didn't touch the concrete foundation of the boardinghouse—if that was the trigger."

Jeremiah drew his brows together. "You did not touch any structure?"

Josie knew she was right! She trusted Jeremiah instinctively, and even he was surprised.

"Nope!" she said, shaking her head. "Will lost his balance and touched the foundation, and I grabbed him to keep him from falling."

Jeremiah nodded. "Well then, that probably explains it. I think it likely that Kaskade chose both of you."

"Nope!" Josie said more firmly, disappointed in his pat response. "Not me."

"As you like," Jeremiah said. His lips twitched, and Josie shook her head again.

"I don't want to hurt anyone's feelings," Will said, "but I'm not ready to get married. Martha's a nice girl—beautiful, in fact—but I don't know her. I don't even know how I'm going to make a living for the next year, much less take care of a wife!"

Leigh murmured a sympathetic sound.

"Do not think about it now," Jeremiah said. "Nothing is set in stone. You may return to your own time—we believe that is where you would go—next year on the summer solstice. If you feel trapped by Kaskade, you will despise your time here. Do not worry about this 'theory.' It is only that, nothing more."

"On the upside, I don't think Martha or Jefferson want to marry anyone either!" Leigh chirped, as if she had said a wonderful thing.

Josie's heart didn't jump...not one little bit.

CHAPTER SEVEN

Jefferson arose the next morning feeling out of sorts. Martha had been uncommunicative on the walk home, stating that nothing was wrong when asked. He was unused to glumness from her, and he had not known how to speak to her. She had prepared dinner, and he had helped her clear the table and wash dishes, which he admitted was unusual for him. He wondered if she was angry with him, but she said not.

As if living with a newly moody sister were not disturbing enough, Jefferson's dreams had been disturbing, largely involving a petite auburn-haired woman floating through the air—perhaps in time—in voluminous skirts too long for her small frame.

The face of the ethereal creature had been Josie's, though her expression had been anything but angelic—instead her lovely dark brows had drawn together in a nervous scowl. Josie's nervous temperament was not suited to the eccentricities of time travel, and he hoped her year in Kaskade passed quickly for her sake, perhaps for his sake as well, as he was not about to propose marriage to a strange young woman. He had come to believe in the notion that Kaskade sought to replenish itself with people from the future, and he had been inclined to believe that those who found the time travelers were destined to fall in love with them.

However, Jefferson no longer believed such nonsense. He would not be marrying Miss Josie Brookman. He would not be marrying anyone, but most definitely not the anxiety-ridden young woman who reminded him of his mother.

He washed and dressed with care, though he had no appointments that day given that it was Saturday. He descended the stairs and stepped into the kitchen to see if Martha was still in a mood.

"Good morning," he said, watching her move about the kitchen. "Would you like some help?"

Martha whirled around, her eyes wide. "What has gotten into you, Jefferson?" she asked. "You rarely help in the kitchen, and now you've offered help twice in twelve hours?"

Jefferson reared his head at her brusque tone. "I beg your pardon! I recently realized that I do not help you out at the house as much as I should."

Martha shook her head and turned toward the stove to stir oatmeal in a pot. "Why do you have this sudden domestic desire, dear brother? Could a petite young woman from the future have inspired you?"

"What?" Jefferson snapped, aghast at her implication. "Why would you say that? What could Josie possibly have to do with my wishing to help you around the boardinghouse?"

Martha shook her head. "I have no idea, but you have been a bit odd since her arrival."

"And you have been a bit odd since Will arrived," he retorted.

"Touché, Jefferson." She seemed not at all troubled by his comment.

"Martha," Jefferson began. "Do not tell me that you are infatuated with that young man."

She set the spoon down and looked over her shoulder. "Infatuated is a strong word, Jefferson."

He watched as she opened the stove and retrieved a pan of biscuits.

"Martha?" he pressed. "That was not an answer. You cannot seriously be enamored of a man whom you just met! Do not fall prey to this romantic fantasy regarding Kaskade!"

Martha twirled around. "Jefferson Lundrum! How dare you! I am not falling prey to anything. I am not enamored of Will Wright. I like him very well, but I am not infatuated or enamored. Further, I do not think this is your business. You have your own concerns, and I think you should confine your attention to those."

"What concerns?"

"Miss Josie Brookman, brother."

"Do not be ridiculous! I could not possibly find myself attracted to such a neurotic young woman. Not at all! Do you forget our mother?"

Martha's angry shoulders slumped. "Jefferson," she remonstrated softly. "Josie is nothing like our mother. And mother was not always neurotic. She only became so in later years."

"I recently recollected the same thing. Nevertheless, those years were enough to convince me that I could only ever imagine marrying someone who worried about nothing, who feared nothing, who viewed life with joy and élan! *Not* that I can imagine marrying at all."

Martha regarded her brother with a return of her usual serene expression. "So we are agreed that neither of us plans to marry the time travelers?"

"Marry?" a female voice said from the open doorway. "What are time travelers?"

Jefferson drew in a sharp breath. He did not realize he had left the kitchen door open, and Mary Woodhouse entered the kitchen. A lovely young brunette woman who was studying to become a nurse, she had come down from Tacoma for the weekend to visit her mother.

"Is someone getting married?" she asked with a sparkle in her brown eyes. "Martha? You?"

"No, no, dear. Not I. Nor Jefferson. We were just chatting about people traveling through Kaskade."

"How do you mean...traveling? Do you mean the itinerants in the lumber camps?"

"Exactly!" Jefferson said. "How are you finding school?"

Crisis averted, Martha returned to cooking.

"Oh, very exciting!" Mary responded. "We are learning all sorts of things. I am sure I will not be able to remember everything I learn."

"Of course you will," Jefferson said. "You are a very smart young lady."

"I certainly hope so. I shall need it!" She turned to Martha. "Could I take mother's tray up to her?"

Mary's mother, an infirm woman, took her tray in her room as a rule, an additional duty that Martha had performed since Mary had moved up to Tacoma to attend nursing school the year before.

"Oh yes! Thank you, Mary," Martha said. "That would be a great help." She set up a tray for Mrs. Woodhouse, and Mary departed with it.

"We have to be more careful," Martha said, closing the door behind Mary. "We have grown lax since Emily stopped coming here."

"Yes, I agree. Now, what can I help you with?"

Martha chuckled. "Jefferson Lundrum, I do not know what has gotten into you, but yes, thank you. Please take these biscuits into the dining room."

Several hours later, breakfast concluded and dishes washed, Jefferson offered to accompany Martha down to the market to pick up fresh vegetables for dinner.

"And now you are coming to the market with me?" she asked while peering into the hall mirror to straighten her hat. "What has this world come to?"

"Do not exaggerate, dear. I have accompanied you to the market before."

"Last year, Jefferson. Once."

"Truly? Just once?"

"Well, to your credit, you are a busy man."

They left the house and turned toward the center of town, strolling along a boardwalk in perpetual need of repair, an ironic state of affairs for a timber mill town.

"I cannot be that busy!" In truth, Jefferson could not remember the last time he had stepped into the mercantile. He had been in the habit of telling Martha if he was in need of anything, such as shaving cream or razors.

A wagon passed them, reminding Jefferson that he probably needed to take a ride soon, perhaps up to the larger town of Orting. His horse, a large sturdy bay, was stabled with the blacksmith, Frank Davis, on the eastern end of town nearest the boardinghouse. Jefferson had not taken the horse out in a week, and Frank certainly didn't have time to exercise all the horses in his stable.

He wondered if Josie rode, but then shook his head. Given her nervous disposition, that was unlikely. Martha did not ride though either, however. She herself had fretted that horses were too big to control.

They turned the corner onto Main Street, the road housing the mercantile, pool hall, a small hotel and various other modest establishments. His own office was nearby on the second story of a false-fronted wooden building housing the bank.

He looked toward the windows of his office, then back at the mercantile. Martha must have caught his glance.

"Jefferson, you can go to your office if you want. You do not have to come to the store with me."

"Nonsense, sister!" he said with feeling. "I said I would come, and I am here!"

"Yes, well, you are not going to actually help me shop, are you? For you have no idea what I want to make for dinner or what things I would need for the house."

"Certainly not!" he said with a chuckle. "I would not *think* of helping you. If you would be so kind as to allow me to carry your purchases home, I would be mostly humbly grateful."

The street seemed particularly busy that morning with wagons, riders on horseback and pedestrians. To reach the boardwalk, Martha and Jefferson crossed between traffic and threaded their way between two wagons parked in front of the mercantile.

Martha paused and turned toward one of the wagons. "Josie!" she said in delight.

Jefferson whirled around to see Josie standing near the head of one of the horses, her hands clasped tightly behind her back, as if she hid them.

"Martha!" Josie exclaimed, turning to greet them. "Hello, Jefferson."

Josie's transformation into a twentieth-century lady was remarkable, dressed as she was in a fetching pink-beribboned sailor hat, silk ivory shirtwaist and a rose taffeta skirt that stopped just above the toes of a black pair of dainty ladies' boots. Lovely curls nestled against the high lace neck of her collar, as if a few errant strands had fallen from the elegant bun at the back of her head.

"Good morning, Josie," Jefferson said.

"What are you doing here?" Martha asked, turning to look toward the door of the mercantile. "Is Will with you? Leigh? You look absolutely lovely, Josie! Is that Leigh's clothing? It fits you so much better than my skirt did."

Josie's cheeks blushed a becoming shade similar to the ribbons on her hat. "Thank you! Will is inside with Leigh. Leigh just bought this outfit this morning for me, as well as some other things that are being delivered to the house. I'll make sure to return your clothing to you as soon as possible. Thank you so much for the loan, Martha! I've had enough of stores and wanted to wait out here. They're very cramped, aren't they?"

"Are they?" Martha asked in a bemused tone as she looked toward the store. "We shall soon find out."

"Like I said, Will and Leigh are inside. They're looking for some things for him. The dressmaker didn't have cufflinks or socks."

"No, I suppose she might not," Martha said. She turned to enter, but Jefferson did not think he could leave Josie standing outside alone.

"Unless you need me inside, Martha, I will wait out here with Josie. I do not like to leave her standing by herself."

"Oh, don't worry about me," Josie said, though her voice did not hold the blithe note she seemed to attempt. "I'll be fine out here."

Jefferson grinned. "I came to help Martha carry purchases home. I would be of little use to her inside the store."

He nodded to Martha, who stepped into the store.

"I'm really all right out here by myself, Jefferson," Josie said.

Jefferson dropped his eyes to the white knuckles of her clasped hands.

"Would you like to sit?" he asked, nodding toward an iron-backed wooden bench near the storefront. "It is not often that this bench is vacant. Some of our older gentlemen enjoy sitting here watching the world go by."

"Sure," Josie said.

Jefferson sat down next to her, noting that the tension in her clasped hands had not eased. He resisted the urge to cover her hands with his own, as if his touch would calm her. He did not feel as if he could speak to her openly, yet knew he must. He spoke in a hushed voice.

"I see that you are distressed about something, Josie. Perhaps your first foray into public? If there is anything I can do to ease your mind, please let me know."

Her next words took his breath away.

"It's not this," she said, nodding in the direction of the street. "It's this love-romance-marriage-destiny thing. I just want to be friends. Please tell me that I don't have to marry you."

CHAPTER EIGHT

Josie heard Jefferson draw in a sharp breath, and she swung her head to look up at him.

"I'm sorry!" she rushed in. "I didn't mean it to sound like that. It's just that I know you don't want to get married. Even Leigh reassured me of that, so I want to take the pressure off...of both of us. I don't know about you, but I don't do well under pressure. I didn't mean to be rude."

Jefferson looked away from her toward the street, where a wagon drove by. A muscle ticked in his jaw, and Josie wondered if she had angered him. While she had been nervously inarticulate, she didn't think she'd said anything insulting.

"Jefferson?" she prompted.

He glanced down at her from under lashes surprisingly dark in a fair-haired man.

"You certainly spoke your mind," he said finally.

"I do that when I'm nervous."

He nodded and turned to look at the street again. "I am aware of your anxious disposition. My mother had similar traits."

"Traits?"

"Yes, she too fretted about a great many things."

"Well, I don't know that I 'fret,' per se."

"No?" He looked down at her, a corner of his mouth twitching, as if he wanted to chuckle.

"Okay, fine! I fret...like your mother. All the more reason we're not destined to marry each other."

"All the more reason," Jefferson repeated, looking away again.

Josie winced at the painful knot in her chest and wondered if it was some form of heartburn. She wasn't prone to heartburn but suspected that had to be the origin of the sensation.

"Right," she murmured, following Jefferson's gaze toward the street.

They fell silent for a few moments, and the awkward quiet nagged at Josie to do or say something. Out of the corner of her eye, she saw a man and woman approaching along the boardwalk. She pulled her feet under her skirt, assuming they would pass by, but they paused in front of the bench.

"Jefferson!" the woman said. "I cannot believe that I see you lounging in front of the mercantile. You are always so busy!"

Jefferson jumped up to greet the tall raven-haired woman wearing a stunning ivory lace blouse and lavender skirt. Her black hat featured matching purple satin ribbons. Josie could have sworn that her sparkling eyes were a shade of amethyst as well. She appeared to be in her early thirties. The gentleman with her, older by about ten years, doffed his charcoal-gray derby and nodded at them, his eyes lingering on Josie.

"Belinda!" Jefferson said, rising quickly. He took her extended gloved hand. "I did not know you had come back to town. How long are you here for?"

He nodded to the gentleman at her side. "Collin, you did not tell me that your sister was coming to visit."

Josie blinked. Belinda seemed much younger than Collin. She would not have suspected they were siblings.

"Do not blame Collin, Jefferson," Belinda said with a lovely laugh. "I surprised him. I do not know how long I will stay. And who is this?"

Belinda turned her dazzling eyes onto Josie, who wished she were anywhere else. She should have expected that Jefferson might have to introduce her to people passing by. The town was small. Everyone probably knew everyone!

She resisted the urge to stand up and curtsey to the tall regal woman.

"Josie, this is Miss Belinda Hutchins and her brother, Collin Hutchins. Collin is an architect and has offices across the hall from mine in the building across the street. Belinda grew up here in Kaskade but moved to Chicago. We do not see her very often."

Josie wondered if that was a note of regret she heard in Jefferson's voice.

Belinda offered Josie her hand, and Josie rose to shake it.

"This is Miss Josie Brookman, who has come to live with us from Seattle."

Josie noted that Jefferson didn't elaborate.

"Oh! Seattle. Such a lovely city," Belinda said. "You are at the boardinghouse then? What brings you to Kaskade?"

Josie's eyes widened, and she started to stammer some kind of response. Martha emerged from the store in a flurry of skirts, and Josie wondered if she had seen them from the window and come to the rescue.

"Belinda! How very nice to see you!" Martha said in a breathless voice. "Good morning, Collin."

Martha leaned forward to kiss Belinda's cheek. Both tall women, they carried themselves with equal elegance.

"I see that you have met Miss Brookman," Martha said. "Josie has come to stay with Dr. Cook and his wife, Leigh. You will not have met Leigh, Belinda. She is just inside with their other guest, Mr. William Wright. Josie and Will are visiting Kaskade for a while. You thought perhaps you might be here a year, is that not right, Josie?"

Josie nodded. "A year," she repeated faintly.

"Do you have family here? Or..." Belinda left the question dangling.

"No, no family," Josie murmured. "My parents passed away."

"Oh, that is too bad," she responded, her sympathy seeming very genuine. "Our parents passed on as well." She looked at her brother, who still studied Josie with unabashed interest.

"It is very nice to meet you, Miss Brookman," Collin said. He did not offer his ungloved hand but nodded in her direction.

"Nice to meet you," Josie said. She would have corrected him to say "Josie" but chose not to make it an issue. She wasn't sure she would run into them again, so it didn't seem to matter.

"What is this about Dr. Cook and his wife?" Belinda asked Martha. "Surely our perennial bachelor doctor has not married?" Her smile verged on a chuckle. She seemed a happy sort of person, just the sort of woman Jefferson might like. Josie thought Jefferson's gaze at Belinda bordered on adoration.

"Yes, Jeremiah married two years ago. They have a child now."

Belinda looked at her brother. "Collin, you never told me that!"

"I did not think to tell you, my dear."

Josie studied Collin more closely. He appeared to be in his early forties, with strands of white appearing at the temples of his black hair. His eyes, like his sister's, were almost purple, like amethysts. Tall and slender, he wore a well-cut handsome charcoal-gray suit and pale-yellow vest. She didn't see a wedding ring on his left hand.

"Here are Leigh and Will!" Martha exclaimed softly.

Josie swore she heard a catch in Martha's voice, but whether from appreciation of Will in a well-fitting camel-brown pinstriped suit or whether Martha was nervous about introducing yet one more time traveler, Josie couldn't guess.

Leigh nodded politely as she and Will stepped up to the group.

"Leigh, this is Miss Belinda Hutchins, who has come to visit her brother, Collin Hutchins," Martha said. "You may know Collin, who has offices in the same building as Jefferson."

"I have met Collin. How are you?" Leigh said, nodding. "It is so nice to meet you, Belinda. Where are you visiting from?"

"I live in Chicago now. I moved away from Kaskade about seven years ago to attend art school, and I never returned."

"Art school?" Leigh echoed. "Are you an artist?"

"I try," Belinda said with a good-natured laugh. "And this must be Mr. William Wright?"

"How did you—" Leigh looked at Martha. "Oh! Martha mentioned Will. Yes, this is Will. Will and Josie are staying with..." Leigh faltered and looked at Martha again.

"I mentioned that Josie and Will are staying with you and Jeremiah for a year or so," Martha supplied.

"Hello, Will," Belinda said, holding out her hand again. Will took it, seemingly as mesmerized by Belinda as Jefferson was.

"Hello," he said simply.

"What brings you to Kaskade?"

Will gave his newly slicked-back hair a slight shake as he shot a glance in Josie's direction. She suspected he was trying to think of an answer. She had no idea what to say. They hadn't really worked on an "origin story."

"Josie and I—" He paused and scanned everyone's faces. "And Leigh are cousins. Leigh told Josie and me so much about Kaskade that we were thinking about moving down here."

Josie quirked an eyebrow but gave Will an approving nod. "Yes," she affirmed to no one in particular.

"A family affair!" Collin said with a smile. "And where do you normally live?"

"Seattle," Josie answered. "We live in Seattle." Will actually lived a little farther south in a town called SeaTac, created around the Seattle-Tacoma airport. She was certain SeaTac had not existed in 1910.

Will glanced at her and nodded.

"I am so pleased to meet everyone," Belinda said. "So much has changed since we sold our parents' house and I went away. Kaskade has grown tremendously, and there are many new people to meet. I do wish I could have you over for dinner, but I am staying with my brother in his rooms at the hotel. They were full, but they kindly brought in a cot for me, just for a few days." She placed a gentle hand on Martha's arm. "I did inquire about room at the boardinghouse but was told you were full?"

Martha tsked. "We are full, but we may have a vacant room next week."

"Truly?" Belinda gasped. "That would be wonderful! I would be willing to wait for a room."

Josie watched as Martha chewed on her lower lip.

"Will your stay here be temporary, Belinda? We normally reserve our rooms for those who need long-term lodging."

"Oh!" Belinda's pale cheeks bloomed. "I truly could not say right now. No matter. I am certain something will open up at the hotel soon."

"I am so sorry," Martha said, her own embarrassment evident.

Josie had thought of the boardinghouse as a fairly large and utilitarian bed and breakfast, but apparently Martha saw it as a home and was unwilling to entertain short-term guests.

"Why don't you join us for dinner?" Leigh said. "All of you. Tomorrow night?"

Josie gasped inwardly. What was Leigh thinking? Josie felt sick at the thought of chitchatting about early-twentieth-century stuff for the length of a dinner.

"That would be lovely," Belinda said with a dazzling smile.

"I do not think I can attend, Leigh, but I am certain that Jefferson could," Martha said.

Josie noted that Jefferson shifted from foot to foot, and she imagined he wasn't very happy with Martha's arrangements for him. Josie imagined he wasn't particularly interested in attending a dinner that she was at, but didn't he want to see Belinda again?

"Can't you find someone to cook dinner tomorrow night, Martha?" Leigh asked. "No one in that house cooks but you?"

"No, I am afraid not," she said. "I could have asked Mary Woodhouse, but I believe she returns to school tomorrow."

"Oh, I'm so sorry!" Leigh said.

"I hear the regret in my sister's voice," Jefferson said. "If you could delay dinner until about eight o'clock, I will help her cook an early dinner for the boarders, and then we can clean up and come to you by eight?"

"Jefferson!" Belinda exclaimed. "What a wonderful brother you are! I did not remember you as being so domesticated."

Josie crossed her arms, certain that Jefferson was just trying to impress Belinda. She wondered if they had a romantic history. They seemed perfect for each other—both tall and elegant, one dark, one light.

"I too had no notion that you helped Martha around the house," Collin said with a wry smile. "You are usually at the office so late in the evenings."

"I confess that I am not the most helpful brother for my sister, but I intend to change my ways."

Jefferson's grin in Belinda's direction brought on the odd sensation that Josie thought might be heartburn again. She patted at her upper chest and cleared her throat. In doing so, all eyes turned on her, as if she had something to say. She had to say something.

"I'd be happy to come help, Martha. I can walk back to the house with you when we're done."

"Goodness! I cannot impose on you like that, Josie. You have just arrived!"

"I don't mind," Josie said. "That way you can come to dinner. I'd be happy to see you there. We all would."

"How nice of you, Josie!" Leigh said.

"I can help too," Will said, obviously not to be outdone. "I'm pretty handy in a kitchen."

"You are?" Josie asked, turning to eye him.

Will's cheeks brightened. He had kept his dark beard, but it had been trimmed down.

"I can help," he repeated.

"Thank you!" Martha said. She turned to Leigh with an embarrassed smile. "It seems that we will be able to attend. For now, I must finish my shopping and return to the house in time for tonight's dinner. It is so nice to see you again, Belinda, Collin. I will see you tomorrow night."

She nodded and turned to walk into the mercantile.

Jefferson tipped his hat. "I think I had better help Martha. I look forward to seeing everyone tomorrow night then."

Josie turned to watch him walking into the store. She couldn't help but admire the cut of his suit, and she supposed he had his suits tailored. Will's suit had been available as ready to wear with just a slight alteration to hem the trousers. Jefferson's shoulders were quite broad, tapering to a trim waist, and Josie imagined he might have trouble finding ready-to-wear clothing that fit so well.

She heard the general hum of conversation around her but jumped when a male voice spoke near her ear.

"Jefferson is a fine-looking gentleman, is he not?"

Josie whirled around to see Collin standing next to her. Beyond him, Leigh and Belinda continued to talk while Will watched and listened, his eyes seemingly riveted to Belinda's face.

"Oh, sure!" she said as nonchalantly as she could. "He's a very nice man."

"He is," Collin said with a wry smile that amplified the attractive dimple in his chin. "I have known him for a very long time."

Josie could have sworn Collin's meaning went deeper than his words.

"Really?"

"Yes, we went to school together."

Josie blinked and studied his silvering hair again.

"Not as children?"

Collin's smile widened. "Yes, actually. You are staring at my white hair. I am afraid my father was completely white by the time he turned forty-five, and I take after him."

Josie's cheeks burned. "I'm sorry. Yes, I did think you were older than Jefferson. I'm really so sorry."

"No need," Collin said. "It is a common mistake."

"So you and Jefferson went to school together," Josie repeated, hoping to change the subject. She looked at Collin from under her lashes, trying to change her previously ingrained image of him as middle aged. He had no wrinkles around his amethyst eyes, no sagging beneath his dimpled chin, no thinning of his thick hair. He held himself erect, and she wondered how she thought he was so much older than his sister.

"Yes. Jefferson was always very popular. He made friends easily. The girls adored him, each wishing that she could become Mrs. Jefferson Lundrum."

Josie raised her head and gave him a direct look. "I can see why they would, but I hope you don't think I'm one of those 'girls.' I don't want to be anyone's 'Mrs.' anything or another."

"No?" Collin asked, turning his gaze on the mercantile door.

"No."

"Good!" Collin surprised her by saying. "I wonder then if you would care to accompany me on a carriage ride sometime in the near future? I could show you more of Kaskade, or perhaps we could lunch in Orting?"

"I...I..." Josie stuttered. His invitation was akin to going out in a car with someone she didn't know. She didn't care what century it was.

"I don't know you!" she exclaimed, albeit in a hushed voice. "I can't just go out to the boonies with you."

He reared his head for a moment before shaking it. "The boonies?"

"The boondocks, out in the wilderness."

"I was not planning on taking the carriage to the wilderness, Miss Brookman, but if you would care for a chaperone, I believe we could attempt to find a suitable lady. Perhaps Mrs. Cook would care to accompany us." He drew his brows together and turned to look over his shoulder. "Or I suppose I could ask Belinda. She would dominate the conversation, of course. That is her way."

Josie followed his eyes. Belinda was certainly hard to miss. She returned her attention to him. His face took on a subtle air of disappointment.

"I understand completely if you do not wish to accompany me on an outing." He looked toward the mercantile. "I may have misunderstood your affection for Jefferson."

"What? No! I have no 'affection' for Jefferson." Out of the corner of her eye, Josie noted Belinda watching them. "If anything, I think he's got a crush on your sister. Will too!"

Collin's lips curved into another wry smile as he looked over his shoulder toward Belinda.

"I believe he did as a youngster, but then she moved away. The bright lights of the big city called to her. She is at present undecided as to her future, but I do not believe she will stay in Kaskade. She has wanderlust. I think she has mentioned San Francisco."

"Oh!" Josie said. "Too bad for Jefferson."

"Or your cousin, for that matter."

"Or Will," Josie said with a smile. "Though he seems very taken with Martha as well."

"As anyone would be. She is a lovely girl."

"She is," Josie agreed.

"Tomorrow night then," they heard Belinda say.

Collin leaned in. "That is my signal. I believe we are about to enter the mercantile. I do not look forward to the experience. I find these stores very confined. I hate to admit to such a frailty, but I tend to become anxious in such crowded spaces."

"Me too!" Josie whispered conspiratorially. "I understand how you feel. That's why I was out here!"

"Ah! You do understand. I see that. I would just as soon visit with you out here while Belinda goes inside, but I see that your cousins are ready to leave." He took her hand and inclined his head over it.

"I look forward to seeing you tomorrow night."

"Won't that make you nervous as well? All those people in a dining room?"

"I imagine it will," he said, "but you will be there. I shall focus on you and your beautiful hazel eyes."

Josie caught her breath. "Oh!"

CHAPTER NINE

"Leigh," Josie began as they walked back toward the house. "How did you ever find the courage to be so social? Especially as a time traveler?" She walked between Leigh and Will.

"Josie!" Will remonstrated.

"No, that's okay, Will. I know exactly what Josie means, and I know you weren't thrilled to hear me invite everyone for dinner. The truth is..." Leigh stopped talking for a moment.

Josie and Will waited expectantly.

"The truth is...I don't know why I invited everyone. Jeremiah will take up the social burden. He can do that. I feel pretty comfortable around Martha and Jefferson. I have no earthly idea why I invited Belinda and Collin. I don't consider myself a very social person either, and honestly, I worry about making mistakes. It's just when Belinda said something about wishing she could invite everyone to dinner, I just came up with this crazy plan. Mrs. Jackson is going to suffer the brunt of my impulsivity. She's the one who has to do all the cooking, but I bet she will look forward to the challenge."

Leigh lifted her eyes from the dusty road and turned to Josie. "Oh, by the way, that was very nice of you to offer to help Martha. I don't think she gets out for dinner much. Emily helped her last year, but she's got a baby now, so can't help anymore. I'm sure Martha can't afford to hire someone. At any rate, thank you. I don't know Belinda, and I barely know Collin. I'll enjoy dinner a lot more if Martha and Jefferson can come."

"No problem," Josie said. She turned to look at Will, uncharacteristically quiet. His new suit flattered him, and she had to admit that she enjoyed his groomed hair. He could not have worn a derby hat on his formerly unruly mop of brown curls. He had not given up his hiking boots despite the store owner's protestations that they would ruin the line of his trousers, but he had allowed Leigh to purchase a pair of wingtip shoes "just in case."

"Is everything all right, Will?" Josie asked. They had turned onto Lakefront Lane, the road bordering the lake.

"Yeah," he said. "Just kind of taking stuff in."

"I noticed you ogling Belinda," Josie said. For some reason, she didn't mind poking fun at Will. Maybe they really were cousins in another life.

"Oh please," he said, his cheeks reddening. "She is beautiful though, isn't she? Like a porcelain doll."

"Hmmpf," Josie murmured. "If you like the raven-haired type. Personally, I think Martha is much more beautiful."

"I agree," Leigh said. "Martha is exquisite really, like an ethereal angel. Jefferson is a masculine version of her."

"Oh, I agree too," Will said with a grin. "Martha is great. Kind of motherly though, isn't she?"

Josie gasped and stopped short. "You're kidding, right? Motherly? You don't mean matronly, do you? Because there's nothing matronly about her."

"No, no, not like that," Will said hastily. "I just meant she's nurturing. You know, she takes care of a boarding house, feeds everyone, cleans up after everyone, and then starts all over again. Really domestic."

"She is, Will," Leigh said. "But there's something in your tone that sounds like you think that's a bad thing."

"No, not bad!" Will protested. "Everyone has a place in this world, don't they? The domestic people, the adventurers, the travelers."

Josie thought she knew where Will was headed. "You're an outdoorsy guy, and you wonder how Martha can stay cooped up in a house all day long?"

Will's shoulders slumped. "It's hard arguing with women," he mumbled. "Yes, I guess that's probably where I was coming from. I couldn't imagine being tied down to a house like that...even finding it hard to go out to dinner or something."

"It's how she makes her living," Josie said softly. "She might want to be adventuring or traveling or painting in San Francisco. We don't know."

"Painting in San Francisco? Where did that come from?" Will asked.

"It was random," Josie replied with a shrug. "Collin said that Belinda was contemplating her future, and he mentioned San Francisco. It had no place in this conversation."

Privately, Josie disagreed with her own statement but felt she had crossed a line. Collin might not like that she had shared a confidence. Belinda might not like it.

"So she's not staying here?" Will asked.

"I don't know," Josie said, hoping to change the subject. "We're almost there!" she exclaimed, spotting the house.

The following afternoon, Josie set out for the boardinghouse, carrying a cloth sack holding the clothing Martha had loaned her. She had just reached the gate when she heard Will call out to her.

"Hey! You're heading for the boardinghouse, right? I thought I was going too."

Josie turned to look at him. He had already started dressing down, shunning a jacket and hat. His white long-sleeved shirt was open at the collar, and the sleeves rolled up to his elbows. He wore no vest, and apparently he had purchased suspenders the day before, because he sported a bright-red pair over his shirt. His slicked-back hair still gleamed, but Josie wondered if it was just wet versus groomed with pomade. Of course he wore his hiking boots.

"Well, you have certainly scaled back on the turn-of-the-century-clothing thing. How long will it be before you cut your pants off above your knees?"

Will chuckled and pushed open the gate.

"Not long if I have my way. I'm thinking of cutting the sleeves of the shirts off too. Here, let me carry that."

Josie rolled her eyes and let him take the bag. "So you're really coming to help cook? Are you really good in the kitchen?"

"I am *not*," Will said firmly. "But I have to do something. I might see if I can get a job in the timber mill."

"Are you kidding?" Josie asked, walking alongside him on Lakefront Lane.

"Why not? Tree conservation is more my thing, but when in Kaskade, do as the Kaskadians do, I guess. I need a job, and I need to do something. I've been doing almost nothing since breakfast. I took a walk down to the lake, cruised around town a little, but I wanted to do it in a covert way. Ya know, I'm not sure I pass for contemporary 1910."

"You did yesterday," Josie said with a laugh. She surveyed him once again. "Actually, you probably do. The suspenders are a nice touch. Very bright."

Will grinned and ran his thumbs under the straps on his chest.

"You like that, huh?"

"Sure, Will." Josie affected a wry tone as she marched on, watching dust swirl around the edges.

"I need to think about a job too," she said. "What can a one-trick librarian do? I could open up a bookshop, but who would front me for that? Or a mobile library, though I'm sure I can't handle a wagon. Or..." She ran out of ideas.

"Do you have any other interests besides books?" Will asked. "I don't think we got to that part of the dating. I know hiking isn't one of your interests."

"And how would I make a living if I liked to hike?"

"I don't know," he said with a shrug. "Tours to the wilderness for city folk?"

"Uh, no," Josie said. "Doesn't even make sense. Who wants to wander around in the wilderness with mosquitoes and things that bite?"

"You'd be surprised, Josie. Actually, you know what? I might skip the timber mill thing and try a guiding service myself. I know my fish. Maybe I can take people out on fishing trips."

They were almost at the end of Lakefront Lane and about to turn toward town. Josie stopped and pointed to more than a few canoes on the lake, fishing poles in the hands of the occupants.

"I'd be surprised if there are any fish left in the lake, Will, but as you can see, everyone seems to know how to fish."

"Oh, I'm sure there are plenty of fish to go around, and I meant I would take city people out, not the local residents. I don't see a sign that says 'Guided Fishing Tours' anywhere!"

"Ever the optimist, Will. Good luck on that."

"Thank you! I'm not sure how I'll fund my first boat, but I'll have to brainstorm that. I guess I could ask Jeremiah for a loan."

Almost at the edge of town, Josie stopped and stared at Will.

"Are you serious? You're going to ask Jeremiah for a loan? Is that really how you want to start this time traveling year in Brigadoon?"

"Brigadoon?"

"An old musical, probably not your thing. It's about a town that appears only once every one hundred years."

"Well, that sounds pretty close to what this is all about."

"It was just a Broadway musical and movie. Anyway, I have to say that I can't believe you're going to bum money from Jeremiah. We just got here! We don't want to look like mooches."

Will started walking again, and with a hand on her hat and another handful of skirt, Josie trotted to catch up.

"Wait!"

Will didn't slow, but he did speak. "You know, Josie, just because we traveled through time together—by accident—doesn't mean you get to tell me how to handle myself, what to do or who to mooch from. Can we agree on that? We'll get along a lot better if we do."

Josie faltered, but Will marched on. She hurried again, wondering if she should take the bag from him.

"Okay," she said in a small voice. She couldn't afford to alienate Will, her only connection to home, and she realized that she had been overbearing. She didn't have the courage to ask anyone for a loan to start a bookshop, but that didn't mean Will couldn't.

"I'm sorry," she said.

Will reduced his speed and looked down at her, the corner of his lips twitching. "You are so bossy!"

"I know," she said. "I have control issues. It's part of my anxiety."

"Why do you have to be anxious? Can't you just stop worrying about things? Especially the ones you can't do anything about?"

Josie grimaced, humiliation pressing on her chest. "I was just born this way, Will. I can't really help it. Don't think I don't try. But let's be honest. Didn't we just travel through time? Weird things do happen that are out of our control. Sure, I'd be anxious!"

Will was silent for a moment, and Josie's natural inclination was to keep pressing her point. Her parents had understood her anxieties, or at least accepted them. The library was a quiet calm place where she rarely felt out of control, but even her coworkers affectionately tolerated her fretful personality. She needed someone on her side in the twentieth century, someone who could understand her and withhold judgment.

They turned the corner toward the boardinghouse, and Josie opened and closed her mouth repeatedly trying to say something to Will that would convince him she was as normal as he—just different. Maybe she was trying to convince herself.

"I don't know, Josie," Will finally said as the boardinghouse came into view. "I still think you can just try to relax a little bit more. I know this is weird, but it's what happened. We can't change it."

Josie swallowed her disappointment. Will didn't seem inclined to simply accept her as she was.

"No, but we can try to figure out why it happened," Josie muttered, almost under her breath.

"Hello," a male voice said nearby.

Josie looked up from studying her feet as she walked. Jefferson approached the boardinghouse from the opposite direction.

"*Both* of you came," he said, coming to a halt at the foot of the steps leading into the house.

"Yeah, I'm going a little stir crazy, so I thought I'd help out," Will said. "I'm actually pretty terrible in the kitchen, but I'll do whatever I can to help. I can wash dishes."

"Welcome to both of you," Jefferson said. "I can cut vegetables and I can wash dishes, so I suppose I shall join you. You look very well, Josie. That color suits you."

Josie looked down at her eggshell muslin blouse and harvest-gold poplin skirt. When they'd purchased it the previous day, Leigh had commented that the color of the skirt matched the highlights in her hair.

"Thank you," Josie said shyly. She preceded the men up the stairs, removing her chocolate-brown satin beribboned sailor hat as she entered the foyer. Jefferson took her hat and hung it on a hook, along with his derby.

"Here are Martha's clothes," Josie said, taking the bag from Will.

"Thank you," Jefferson said. He set the bag down on a chair by the door.

The clanking sound of pots and pans emerged from the kitchen, and they moved in that direction as a group. They stepped in to see Martha scurrying around the kitchen.

"How can I help?" Josie asked.

"Hello! Thank you for coming. Hello, Will. You too? Jefferson, please show them where the aprons are. Josie, could you peel potatoes? Do you know how?"

Josie couldn't help but chuckle as Martha set up a pot for boiling water.

"Yes, I think I can manage to peel potatoes."

Jefferson pulled two aprons off a hook on the back of the kitchen door and handed them to Josie and Will. Will balked but finally accepted the apron and tied it on. Jefferson removed his jacket and loosened his tight collar, hanging both jacket and tie on the same hook.

"Do you have a potato peeler?" Josie looked at the ominous pile of potatoes that needed peeling on the kitchen table.

Martha looked over her shoulder.

"A peeler? Do you mean a knife? Yes, there is a knife right there by the potatoes."

Josie eyed a sharp-looking wooden-handled knife with apprehension. What if she cut herself? Did they have Band-Aids? Antibiotics? She swallowed and set to work hacking at the skin of the potatoes and hoping she didn't cut her fingers off.

Truth be told, Josie wasn't much of a cook. She had volunteered to help Martha with a vague idea of handling some of the cleanup and dishwashing, but the men had jumped on that opportunity. She dearly hoped that Martha didn't turn around and ask her to "toss a salad together." Her idea of cutting vegetables was spooning things from the salad bar at the grocery store near her apartment.

She whacked away at the potatoes silently for a few minutes until Jefferson appeared at her side, taking a potato and the knife from her hands.

"Here," he said in hushed voice. "Cut off the end of the potato and hold it upright like this. Slice off only the skin, directing the knife down on the cutting board. That way you will not cut yourself. You seem to miss this potato peeler you inquired about." He handed the knife back to Josie, who followed his example.

"Thank you," she whispered. "Frankly, I've cut myself with a potato peeler, so that's no help either. This is a pretty nifty trick."

"It is no trick," Jefferson said. "My mother peeled potatoes like this all the time. She was afraid of cutting herself."

"She sounds like my kind of people," Josie mumbled.

"I think perhaps she was," Jefferson said.

To Josie's surprise, he retrieved another knife and started helping her peel potatoes. For all that he said he couldn't cook, he seemed to know his way around the kitchen.

As they stood side by side peeling potatoes, Josie studied his capable hands with their long fingers. Standing so close, she found herself enjoying his scent—a clean soapy smell that surprised her. She knew that Jeremiah and Leigh enjoyed cleanliness, since they lovingly jostled at the end of the hall for the bathroom every morning, but she didn't imagine others might wash every day in 1910. Still, she recalled that Jefferson always smelled fresh whenever she happened to be near him...which wasn't that often.

"What is that scent?" she couldn't help asking. She kept her eyes on her task.

"What scent? I think Martha made biscuits."

"No, I mean, your scent." Josie paused and swallowed hard. That didn't sound right at all. "I mean, your soap. It smells nice. I think I'll ask Leigh to buy some."

"I believe it is called Barber's Bar Soap. I had noted that the smell was a bit strong and thought to discontinue it. Do you really wish to purchase shaving soap for yourself?"

Josie bit her lip. So much for that. "I guess?"

"You guess what?"

"Well, I like the smell, and it doesn't really matter what it's called though, right?" Josie was not about to give in.

"I suppose not," Jefferson said with a chuckle. "Thank you."

"For what?"

"For the compliment about my scent."

"Well, it was really more about the soap. But you're welcome."

"You smell very nice as well," Jefferson murmured.

Josie glanced up in surprise, and she felt the knife cut her index finger. She looked back down to see blood flowing onto the cutting board. Her knees buckled for a moment.

CHAPTER TEN

Jefferson grabbed Josie's hand and held it up. Blood ran down her arm, saturating her sleeve. He pulled her over to the sink and snatched up a clean white dishcloth from a pile Martha kept at the ready.

"What has happened?" Martha cried out, moving to their side.

"Josie has cut herself. I think the wound is quite deep." Jefferson tried to keep his voice calm, though he did not feel so. Josie's face had paled, and she wobbled on her feet.

"Can you support her, Martha? She seems faint."

Martha slid her arm around Josie's waist while Jefferson bound her left index finger as tightly as he could. Blood seeped through the dishcloth, and he knew she needed medical attention.

"We must get her to Jeremiah without delay," he said through clenched teeth.

"Jefferson!" Martha cried out. "I cannot hold her. She's slipping!"

Will jumped in to grab Josie before she fainted.

"Josie!" he called out, holding her upright as her head lolled against his chest. "Wake up! Come on, girl. It's only a cut!"

"Will, it is far more serious than that," Jefferson snapped. "Your words are unhelpful."

Will looked up. "She gets anxious like this. She probably just stopped breathing or something. People do, and then they faint."

"Take her hand and hold it high, Martha! Release her, Will. You really do not know what you are talking about. She may be going into some sort of shock."

Will let go and stepped back with a shake of his head while Jefferson scooped Josie up into his arms. Martha took Josie's hand and held it high.

"Tie her wrist around my neck, Martha."

"I don't understand," Martha gasped. "Why?"

"To keep her hand up while I carry her to Jeremiah's house. Quickly now. Use a towel."

Martha did as he asked and stepped back, wringing her hands.

"Jefferson, let me hold her arm up while you carry her," she said.

"Too impractical, dear. We could never move quickly enough. I must go. Stay here and care for the boarders."

"Blood is running down your collar, Jefferson," Martha whispered.

"It does not matter."

"That *is* a lot of blood," Will exclaimed. "Maybe she is going into shock, as you say. I'll run ahead and let Jeremiah know you're coming. Do you have a wagon or something?"

"No time to fetch a wagon or my horse." Jefferson grunted under Josie's weight as he hurried down the hallway.

Will pulled open the door, and they rushed through it.

"I will wait to hear news!" Martha called out from the doorway.

Though Jefferson knew the trip to Jeremiah's house was not long, at that moment it seemed as if it were miles away. Strengthened by his own anxieties for Josie's welfare, he hurried down the road. Will ran past him and disappeared around a corner toward downtown.

Jefferson looked down at Josie's pale face. Gone was the color in her lovely peach cheeks.

"Josie!" he said between ragged breaths. "Josie, wake up!"

Her eyes remained closed, and she seemed hardly to breathe. Jefferson quickened his step. Upon reaching the center of town, he saw Will turn the corner onto Lakefront Lane. Jefferson ignored curious passersby and kept moving.

When he reached Lakefront Lane, he spotted Will at the far end, turning into the picket fence bordering the Cook house. Summoning what little strength he had left, Jefferson lurched forward down the road. Josie was not heavy, but he was not a particularly muscular man. He struggled, fear the only thing that gave him strength.

Jefferson looked up from Josie's face to see Jeremiah racing out of his gate and down the road toward him. Relief swept through him, and he stumbled, recovering without dropping Josie. He saw a large quantity of blood on his shirt, and his fears were renewed.

"Jefferson!" Jeremiah called out.

Will ran closely behind him. In the distance, Leigh hurried toward them.

"She cut her hand," Jefferson panted when Jeremiah arrived at his side. "It seems severe. Please tell me that you can fix it."

"I am sure that we can, Jefferson. Do not fret. Will explained she cut her finger peeling potatoes. Given the amount of blood on your clothing though, the wound may be deep. Let me take her. You look spent."

"No, I have her," Jefferson said. "I will carry her in." He carried Josie to the Cook house, followed by Jeremiah, Leigh and Will. Jeremiah directed him through the parlor to his office and examining room, where he told Jefferson to lay Josie out on a padded steel table covered by a white sheet.

Jeremiah washed his hands in a basin of water with soap and dried them before turning back to Josie.

Leigh hung back at the doorway, and she put a hand on Will's arm when he would enter.

"Let Jeremiah work," she said.

Jefferson had no intention of leaving the room.

"How can I help?" he asked Jeremiah, who carefully pulled the cloth away from Josie's hand.

"Can you cover her with that blanket? And slip another one under her feet." Jeremiah indicated the items in a nearby cupboard.

Jefferson picked up the lightweight white cotton blankets and laid one over Josie before slipping the other folded one under her feet. He stood back to watch as Jeremiah examined Josie's hand. The bleeding had not stopped, and Jefferson swallowed hard.

"This is a deep cut," Jeremiah said. "She will require sutures. Since you are here, I could use your assistance. Bring me that table, then wash your hands in that basin. Then I need you to gather up the necessary items as I point them out."

Jefferson rolled over a metal table holding various bits and pieces of medical paraphernalia, none of which he was particularly familiar with. He followed instructions and washed his hands, following which Jeremiah directed him to a drawer in a cabinet, where he retrieved a kit containing white silk sutures and curved needles. Jeremiah further directed him to produce a bottle of antiseptic and white bandages from other drawers in the cabinet.

"Yes, thank you. Set those on the table there. She is unconscious, so I think I will suture her finger quickly before she awakens. I do not wish to use chlorophyll if not necessary."

Jefferson suspected Jeremiah spoke largely to himself. He watched as Jeremiah cleaned the wound, but Jefferson found himself unaccountably squeamish when Jeremiah began to suture the wound. He turned partially away to see Leigh appeared equally queasy. Will watched with interest, but Leigh turned away. Jefferson checked Josie one more time but knew she was in the best possible hands. He stepped past Will to attend to Leigh.

Lowering her to a seat, he sat down beside her.

"I'm sorry," she said. "I don't normally watch Jeremiah at work. It just brings up all sorts of stuff for me."

"I understand," Jefferson said, covering her hand with his. "I must admit that I felt unwell myself. I did not realize that I was so weak-kneed around injuries."

"Well, maybe you're worried. I know that I am. That was a lot of blood."

"Yes, she cut herself quite deeply. To my great shame, I should have watched her more carefully."

"Why to your shame? Will said she cut herself peeling potatoes?"

"Yes, I was helping. She did seem uncomfortable with the use of a knife. I have noted that she tends to have a nervous disposition."

"Yes, she does, poor thing. It can't be easy. You would think Kaskade would snag people who are better able to handle this sort of thing."

"Perhaps," Jefferson said. "Perhaps Kaskade will be the making of her."

Leigh jerked her head. "What do you mean by that?"

Jefferson wished the words unsaid. "Truthfully, I do not know. Perhaps I was thinking that with Josie's complete immersion into the fearful unknown, she may learn to fear less. It must be exhausting to worry as much as she seems to. I told her that she reminds me of my own mother, who fretted constantly."

"So Josie reminds you of your mother?"

"Yes, I suppose that she does. Not in appearance, mind you, but in temperament. Although to be fair, Martha reaffirmed a memory I had that our mother was not always an anxious person but became so in later years."

Leigh nodded and looked toward the doorway to the office. "Well, Josie is just Josie. I like her. I know she worries a lot, but wouldn't you if you were thrown through time to another century? Say the seventeen hundreds and found yourself trying to decide if you wanted to stay loyal to the English crown or choose a government of the people by the people and for the people?"

Jefferson tilted his head. "When you word it that way, I become anxious myself!" He patted Leigh's hand and rose. "I think I will just look in. I am concerned about the severity of her wound. At one point, I worried that she had lost too much blood."

Leigh rose but did not follow him. "See? Everyone worries. I'd better run into the kitchen and tell Mrs. Jackson that dinner is off. Then I had better send a note to Belinda and Collin to cancel. I don't really feel like socializing right now."

"I had forgotten," Jefferson said. "That was the entire reason Josie was peeling potatoes...to help Martha. I cannot speak for you, but I do not think Martha will be able to get away as well, and I do not think I can be very festive knowing Josie will be in a good deal of pain." He caught his breath. "You do not think she will lose her finger, do you?"

Leigh's eyes widened. "Was the cut that bad?"

Jefferson shook his head. "No, no. It was quite deep, but I do not believe it approached detachment."

He hurried to the door and looked in. Will had entered the room and sat down on a nearby stool to observe. Josie remained unconscious as Jeremiah bandaged her hand. Jefferson moved to Jeremiah's side.

"She is still unconscious," Jefferson said in a low voice. "Is that a problem?"

Jeremiah looked up. "No, I do not believe so. Her skin feels warm. She did not fall and hit her head, did she?"

Jefferson shook his head. "No, we all took hold of her when she fainted."

"Then I see no problem. She is not in shock, which I feared initially. She has lost quite a bit of blood, and I am unsure if she will have full use of the finger. It is possible she cut a tendon. I think I must consult with a surgeon in Tacoma."

Jefferson caught his breath. "A surgeon? For a finger?"

"Yes. She may not be able to bend it in the future."

Jefferson looked over at Will, who grimaced but said nothing.

Josie moaned, and Jeremiah put a hand on her forehead. She opened her eyes.

"Hello, Josie," Jeremiah said. "You are in my office. How do you feel?"

"My hand hurts," she whispered, attempting to raise her arm.

Jeremiah had enveloped the hand in a bandage, and the weight seemed to surprise her. He helped her raise her hand to look at it. The expression of horror on her face startled Jefferson.

"Did you cut my hand off?" she gasped, trying to sit up.

"No, no, dear," Jeremiah said, holding her down. "I only sutured your finger. The bandage is to protect your hand."

"Oh!" she said. "It hurts."

"Yes, I know. I am so sorry. I could give you some laudanum for the pain."

"Laudanum?" she repeated. "No, thank you. That's addictive, isn't it?"

"Yes, one can develop a dependence for it, but it would not hurt to take a teaspoonful for pain."

"No, thank you," Josie said. "Can I sit up?"

She held up her uninjured hand, and Jeremiah helped her rise to a sitting position on the bed. She seemed to see Jefferson standing and Will seated for the first time, and she blinked.

"How did I get here? The last thing I remember is Jefferson dragging me to the sink and wrapping my hand."

"I carried you," Jefferson said simply.

"You're kidding! That must have been a long haul. I'm sorry!"

"There is no need to apologize, Josie!" Jefferson protested. "Why ever would you apologize?"

She shrugged. "Because I feel bad that you carried me all this way. I could probably stand to lose some weight. Was it awfully hard? Was I heavy?"

"Not at all!" Jefferson responded gallantly.

"He hurried down the road carrying you as if you were a feather," Jeremiah said with a smile. "And you do *not* need to lose weight. You are already petite."

Josie blushed and dropped her eyes to her hand. "Do I still have my finger?"

"Yes, though the cut was deep. I would like to consult with a surgeon to see if you cut a tendon. I would not want you to suffer any long-term damage. You mostly likely would not do so in your time given the probable advances in medicine."

"I think that's probably true," Will said quietly.

"A surgeon?" Josie echoed Jefferson. "Oh no! This can wait till I get back, can't it?"

"Do you mean wait until the next summer solstice, when you are first able to return to your own time?" Jefferson clarified.

"Yes. I just cut the darn thing. I don't want a surgeon cutting it again. How hideous!"

"That seems a long time to wait, Josie," Jeremiah said. "The surgery after your finger heals would be much more extensive and complicated."

Josie shook her head emphatically. "I don't want surgery."

"Let us discuss it further at another time. You need to drink something and rest."

"Ohhhh! What about Martha and dinner? Did I ruin that?"

"You did not *ruin* anything, Josie," Jefferson said. "You had an accident. I do believe Leigh intends to cancel the dinner tonight, as neither Martha nor I will be able to attend."

"You won't?" she said in a piteous voice.

Jefferson reared his head. Did she really wish *his* presence?

"I mean...both of you," Josie said. "I'm so sorry. I really feel like I messed things up."

Will rose quickly, impatiently. "Geez, Josie. The world doesn't revolve around you. *You* didn't mess things up. Don't worry about it. It was just dinner."

Josie's face turned bright red, and Jefferson wanted to throttle Will, who turned for the door.

"Glad to see you're on the mend," Will muttered. He left the examining room, and Jefferson turned back to see tears filling Josie's eyes.

"I know the world doesn't revolve around me," she was mumbling to her hand.

"What a strange thing to say," Jeremiah murmured.

"It's a common saying in our time."

"Pay him no mind," Jefferson said. "He was probably distraught about your injury."

Josie looked up with a wry lift of one eyebrow, which struck Jefferson as particularly charming.

"I seriously doubt that Will was 'distraught' over me cutting my finger, but thank you. I think he's fed up with my anxieties. We talked about that this morning."

"Such a shame," Jeremiah tsked sympathetically. He busied himself cleaning up his office.

"I am very sorry," Jefferson said, feeling he must offer some response. "I know you two are close."

Josie narrowed her eyes. "Me and Will? Actually, no, we're not, but I did hope that we could be allies in this time traveling thing since we're in the same boat."

"Allies, of course," Jefferson repeated. "Though I hope you don't see your time here as a battle...well, perhaps any more than you have endured already. I hope you enjoy your time in Kaskade."

Josie held up her hand and grinned, almost lightheartedly. "I'm sure I will. And no, I don't see this as a battle."

"Good!"

"Thank you for helping me," she said. Her eyes mirrored her sincerity.

He had not think her capable of such a direct gaze. "You are most welcome," Jefferson said, drawn into the hazel depths of her eyes. He felt a thump in his chest, then another.

Chapter Eleven

Josie awakened the next morning with a throbbing finger. She contemplated giving in and asking Jeremiah for laudanum for about a minute before she shook her head. After she returned from the bathroom—which was itself difficult to manage—she stopped by the wardrobe, eyeing the clothing that Leigh had purchased for her.

How was she to manage getting dressed? Especially the corset?

A knock on the door brought Leigh into the room, as if she had heard Josie fussing.

"Good morning," she said. "How is your hand?"

"It hurts," Josie said.

"You know that Jeremiah has something for that. Of course, you'll probably be a zombie all day, but your hand won't hurt."

Josie shook her head. "Laudanum, right? That comes from opium, doesn't it?"

"Yes. Jeremiah and I talked about that. There has already been concern about addiction to laudanum and opium within the medical community, and I told him the future isn't promising. He's changed the way he uses laudanum or gives it out. He's very particular and only hands out a bit at a time, but frankly, it's available without a prescription. You and I know that will change, but I'm not sure when. History wasn't my thing."

"You would think I would know since books *are* my thing, but I don't know either. Something about the Food and Drug Act comes to mind."

"Yes, I think that just passed in 1906. Jeremiah has mentioned it. Anyway, okay, so you're going to push through the pain, huh? I know I did with Jeri's birth."

"I think I'll be all right as far as pain goes. Getting dressed...now that's another thing!"

Leigh laughed. "That's why I'm here! To help you get dressed. I suspected it would be hard this morning."

Leigh helped Josie out of her nightgown and into the assortment of clothing necessary to get about in decent fashion in 1910. Josie felt like a child as Leigh tightened her corset and pulled her forest-green skirt up over her hips.

"I'm going to have to figure this out," Josie muttered as Leigh laced up a pair of dark boots. "I can't have you waiting on me hand and foot...literally."

Leigh rose with a chuckle. "You will." She scrunched her forehead. "Though I don't know how. It takes two hands to tie corsets and boots. I really don't mind helping."

"Did Jeremiah say how long I have to wear the bandage?"

Leigh shook her head. "No, but you can ask him this morning. I know he wants to look at it. Any further thoughts on a surgery consult?"

Josie bit her lip and looked at Leigh. "I'd rather wait till I get back. I hope you understand."

Leigh nodded. "I do. I know that health care is better in our time. I don't take it personally. I can understand that you don't want any surgery. Frankly, I hope you heal without any complications!"

"Me too. I was kind of woozy, so I don't know how deep it was, but there you go! Me and knives—not a good thing."

"I'm with you there. Thank goodness for Mrs. Jackson."

They left Josie's bedroom and went down to breakfast. Josie was right handed, so she managed breakfast well enough. When finished, she agreed to follow Jeremiah to his office to be examined. She sat on the examining table while Jeremiah washed his hands before unwrapping the large bandage. He examined the finger gently, though Josie flinched a few times. She kept her eyes on the ceiling, refusing to look at the wound.

"Oh dear," Jeremiah said. "I have started it bleeding again. You do not have hemophilia, do you, Josie?"

"Hemophilia? No!" She looked down at her finger, oozing blood beyond red-stained white stiches. She had expected to see gruesome black stitching and supposed she should be grateful, but her stomach lurched.

"There is no need to panic," Jeremiah said. "It was just an inquiry. Your wound has not clotted yet as I had hoped, but there is no evidence of hemorrhage."

Josie looked up at the ceiling, trying to recall if her parents had problems with bleeding. Both had taken baby aspirin for stroke prevention and tended to easy bruising, but she had never done so.

"Do you think I have hemophilia?" she asked. "Does it look like I do?"

"There is no evidence that you do, Josie. I should be more judicious in my questions. I will just reapply the bandage, and we will not disturb it for several days."

Sweat broke out on Josie's upper lip, and she bit back a cry of pain as Jeremiah wrapped her finger again.

"I am sorry, Josie. I know that hurts. It is, however, good to know that you have sensation in the finger. Have you considered my suggestion for a surgery consult in Tacoma?"

"I don't really want to consider surgery, Jeremiah. Can we wait?"

"Yes, if you wish."

She kept her eyes on the ceiling while he finished wrapping her hand.

"Will approached me this morning asking me to invest in a guide fishing business while he is here. I told him I would consider it. I probably should not ask you this, Josie, but you know him better than anyone. Do you feel he might be a good investment? Does he seem knowledgeable about fishing and guiding?"

"Oh!" Josie exclaimed. "I don't really know, Jeremiah. I honestly don't know Will that well either. He's a fish and wildlife biologist, so he probably does know about fish. Do you think there's a market for a fishing guide service on the lake? It's awfully small."

"Lake Kaskade is much larger than it appears from the northern shore. It extends toward the south for several miles. All that you can see here from town is the width of the lake, which is about half a mile."

"Really? I had no idea."

"I do think it is feasible that Will could earn a modest living if he does indeed understand fish and how to find them. I think I will invest. I know that he wants to earn a living while he is here."

Josie felt the same way, but she wasn't about to ask anyone for a loan. She looked down at her bandaged hand and supposed she couldn't do anything in the near future anyway.

"That's very nice of you, Jeremiah."

Jeremiah helped Josie stand. She wobbled, her finger throbbing up to her wrist.

"Not at all. Do not overexert yourself today, Josie. I am concerned that you seem to be a bit lightheaded."

"I'm just a little woozy from nerves, Jeremiah. I'll take it easy. Thank you."

"My pleasure," he said.

Josie left his office and wandered into the parlor. No one was in there, and she supposed that Leigh was with the baby. She went to the front door and stepped outside with the intention of lounging on the wicker furniture on the porch. The weather was pleasant and unusually dry for Washington State. After about five minutes of enjoying the view of the lake across the road, Josie fidgeted on the love seat, wishing she had brought a book outside to read. She imagined Jeremiah and Leigh probably had more than just medical journals on hand.

"Good morning!" someone called out from the road. Jefferson entered the gate and strode up the walkway. As handsome as ever in a dove-gray pinstriped suit, he removed his charcoal-gray derby as he climbed the steps.

Josie was about to jump up at his arrival, but he stayed her with a gesture.

"May I sit with you?"

"Sure!" she said, more confident than she felt.

Jeremiah sat next to her on the loveseat, dropping his eyes to her hand.

"How are you this morning? I was on my way to the office and thought I might make a detour and inquire after your well-being."

"I'm fine." She wasn't about to tell him how much her hand hurt.

She wished it had just been her finger, but it seemed as if her entire hand throbbed.

"Fine?" he asked. "Your face looks pinched."

"Okay, my hand hurts," she said. "I'm embarrassed I can't be trusted with a kitchen knife."

"I feel terrible that I distracted you when you were cutting potatoes."

"Did you?"

"I think so. I remember that you looked up at me and then cut your hand."

"Hmmm," she murmured. "I don't remember." She breathed in his fresh scent, hoping that he didn't notice.

"Did Jeremiah say how long he thought it might take to heal?"

"No, not really," she said in a bemused voice. Somehow the throbbing in her hand eased. "Getting dressed is a pain."

"Yes, I can imagine it must be painful. Surely someone can help you?"

"Oh, I meant a chore, hard to do, not painful. But yes, Leigh helped me this morning. You all wear a lot more clothing than we do in my time."

Jefferson chuckled. "*You all* do, not I. Ladies do, that is, and that is all I shall say on the subject."

"Gotcha," Josie said. She noticed his cheeks had taken on color, and he seemed to look everywhere but at her. He fell silent for a moment.

"How are you enjoying your stay here with the Cooks?"

"They're very nice. It's a beautiful house, but then the boarding-house looked very nice as well."

He smiled, as if he knew she had added the last statement to appease him.

"And Will? Is he staying busy?"

"Funny that you ask. I don't know if it's my business to say, but I think Jeremiah is going to loan him some money to start a fishing guide business while he's here. So that should keep him busy."

"How interesting!" Jefferson said. "That is very fortunate for Will."

"Yes, indeedy," Josie said, feeling more in tune with Jefferson than she ever had with Will. In fact, she felt positively chatty with

Jefferson at the moment. "Frankly, when he told me he wanted to ask Jeremiah for a loan, I told him I thought it was a bad idea. He put me in my place though."

"Why did you think it was a bad idea? It makes sense. There is nowhere else to which Will could apply for a loan on his own without a guarantor. I take it he would wish to buy a boat and fishing gear."

"I imagine so. Okay, it makes sense, but still, we just got here. I didn't want to give the impression that we were mooching, but I've learned my lesson!" Josie grinned, still amazed that her hand had stopped hurting. "It wasn't my place to tell him what to do."

"No? To be clear, you and Will are not..." He let the question dangle.

"No, we are not. We tried dating a few times, but it wasn't going to work. We're too different. He's pretty laid back and outdoorsy, and I'm a worrywart and happiest with my books."

"You were a librarian, you said."

Josie nodded.

"Do you think you will miss it very much?"

Josie sighed. "I do. If I had my way, I'd open up a little bookshop while I'm here, but that's probably not going to happen. Still, like Will, I do have to find a way to make money. I almost feel like because I'm female, everyone thinks it's okay for me to just live off of Leigh and Jeremiah, but I can't! I have to earn my keep."

Jefferson took hold of her wrist above the bandaged hand that she had waved around as she spoke. He held on to it gently. "Do try to keep your hand still."

"Sorry!" she said. "Funny! It stopped hurting."

"That is good. So you would like to open a bookshop? I can see a need for one here. I believe there is a vacant store near the mercantile. I see it every day from the window of my office."

"Really?" Josie then shook her head. "No, I'm not asking Jeremiah for a loan as well. I think I heard he does a lot of charity work. He's probably not as wealthy as he looks."

"Would you ask me for a loan?" Jefferson asked.

Josie's jaw dropped. "What? No!" she exclaimed. "No!" She tried to raise her hand to ward off the question, but he still held on to her wrist.

"I admit that I do not have much, but I could offer you what I have. It would be enough to rent the store and purchase a limited inventory."

"Oh, Jefferson! Noooo... But thank you! How sweet! And no."

"You are stubborn," he said with a shake of his head.

"That's probably a good thing in this case."

Jefferson fell silent for a moment. "If you will not take the money from me, would you consider applying to the bank for a loan with my co-signature?"

Josie's mouth worked, but words wouldn't come out. When they did, she wasn't too pleased with them. "Are you kidding?" she asked ungracefully. "I mean, really? Why would you offer to do that for a complete stranger, Jefferson?"

"You are *not* a complete stranger, Josie. Further, I believe in you...that is to say, I believe in your genuine desire to seek gainful employment, and there is little to do in Kaskade for someone of your talents. I think it an excellent idea, and should you decide to leave next summer, you could sell the store."

"So you don't mind if I leave next summer?" Josie suppressed a gasp as she blurted out the question.

Jefferson jerked his head to look at her, his eyes wide and inquiring.

"No! That's not what I mean," Josie said hastily. "What I meant to say was that if I leave and can't sell the store, you'd be liable for the rest of the loan. That's a big risk, Jefferson. I've always wanted my own bookstore, but there are reasons why I didn't open one. One is money, and another is competence. You know me by now. You've seen me. Do I look like the kind of person who could run a business? As stressed out as I get?"

Jefferson pressed his lips together, and Josie's heart sunk. Not only was he unconcerned that she might leave, she had just talked him out of his offer. Which she had fully intended to do. So she told herself.

"You must have more confidence in yourself, Josie. I believe I have more confidence in you than you do in yourself. I am fully prepared to take on the responsibility of the bank loan. I am sure you will make payments when you begin to make a profit." He paused, and Josie looked down at his hand on her wrist. "And yes, I do mind if you leave next summer, but that is your decision. I look forward to working with you and hearing about your progress in the store. What shall you name it?"

He finally released her hand, and she felt the loss of his touch.

"I hadn't even thought about it. I haven't even agreed to take you up on your offer."

"But you will," he said with confidence.

Josie melted. She resisted the urge to lean into him and lay her head on his shoulder. "But I will. And I thank you."

His smile was so broad that she basked under its glow.

"What shall you name the store?"

"How about Jefferson and Josie Book Emporium?"

Jefferson laughed, a wonderfully full-bodied sound full of genuine mirth.

"Emporium?" he repeated. "Though I do appreciate the rest of the name. There is no need to include my name."

Josie's smile drooped. "Oh, sorry! You probably don't want your name publicly associated with the store, with me."

"It is not that at all. I think this is your project, and you must claim it as your own. Consider me nothing more than a silent partner...a very silent partner."

"Jefferson and Josie Bookstore then."

"Josie and Jefferson Bookstore."

"Deal!" Josie offered her right hand for a shake, and Jefferson pulled it to his lips before jumping up.

"I must get to the office. Come by today if you can, and we shall go visit the bank."

"So soon?" Josie asked, suddenly shaking, but whether from the kiss to her hand or the speed toward opening a bookstore, she couldn't say.

"Before you change your mind!" With a nod, Jefferson put his hat on his head and strode down the steps. Josie watched in a befuddled trance as he passed through the gate, turned to wave then hurried down the road in the direction of town.

"What just happened?" she whispered aloud, bringing her hand to her lips.

Chapter Twelve

"Leigh, do you know exactly where Jefferson's office is? I'm supposed to go there today. I'm not really sure I had a choice."

Josie had waited several hours before asking the question. She hadn't really wanted to tell anyone at all. In fact, she still debated going down to Jefferson's office, thanking him very much but declining his offer. Except she wasn't sure where his office was.

Leigh, passing in front of Josie's room, paused. Josie had been waiting for her to emerge from the baby's room, where she had put Jeri down for her morning nap.

"Really? Why are you supposed to go there? You're not suing Martha, are you?" She chuckled. "No, really, what's up? And what do you mean you're not sure if you have a choice?"

Josie scanned the hall for anyone listening and then pulled Leigh into the room, shutting the door behind her.

"Okay, I did *not* ask for this. I didn't. Jefferson offered. He—"

"Really?" Leigh interrupted with a squeal. "Really? Oh, I could see he was really bowled over by you, but so soon? Congratulations, Josie! I know you two are going to be so happy. He'll have to move out of the boardinghouse, but yay!" She grabbed Josie for a hug, but Josie struggled out of it.

"Wait! Wait! No! No! He didn't propose! For goodness' sake, Leigh! I hardly know the man!"

Leigh's cheeks reddened. "Oh! Well, what offer did he make? I don't understand."

"He offered to cosign on a loan for me so I can buy a bookstore. He already knows a location for it near the mercantile."

"A bookstore! Does that mean you're staying?"

Josie shook her head. Things were going much worse than she'd expected.

"No," she murmured with a guilty droop of her shoulders. "I just wanted to make money while I was here. You're right. It's foolish to try to start a business in a year and then leave it...or sell it."

"I didn't say that. I just thought—"

"Unless Jefferson takes it over," Josie said. "He could hire someone to run it for him. Since he'll be on the loan, he'll have some say."

"You said Jefferson offered?"

"Yes, I promise. I didn't ask him for money. I mean...he offered money at first, but I refused. Then he suggested cosigning on a loan to lease the store and buy the inventory. What do you think?"

Leigh moved to a chair and dropped down onto it. "Wow! That's a lot to handle in a year. Are you sure you're up for it, Josie?"

Josie locked her knees, shaking from the interaction.

"I suppose you mean, can my nerves handle it?"

Leigh pressed her lips together and eyed her sympathetically. "Yes, that's exactly what I mean. I'm not judging you, Josie. I've never owned my own business, and certainly not in 1910. I imagine it's a lot of stress."

Josie crossed her arms. "Well, as long as there's a bathroom in the store, I guess I'll be fine."

To her surprise, Leigh started laughing.

"You did not just say that!"

Josie's lips widened. "I did. Plus I'm probably serious about that."

"Oh, Josie! I gotta hand it to you. You're brave!"

Josie had been called many things, but brave was not one of them. She blushed and took a chair near Leigh.

"Not hardly, but thank you for the thought. Jefferson said he thought I could handle it. I'm not sure why he thinks that, but I welcome the vote of confidence."

"Well, like I said..." Leigh didn't finish her sentence, but she grinned.

"Like you said what?"

"When I thought he had 'offered' as in a proposal of marriage, I said he was bowled over by you. It follows that he has confidence in your abilities."

"What?" Josie said in surprise. "When did you say he was 'bowled over' by me?"

"Just a few minutes ago."

"Well, that's just nuts! Of course he isn't. Don't you see how irritated he gets when I get stressed out? No, I'm not his cup of tea at all. Besides, he's 'bowled over' by Belinda Hutchins. And who wouldn't be?" Josie's voice dropped an octave.

"I did see him ogling her, but so was Will. She's kind of mesmerizing, isn't she? But you should have seen him when he ran here with you in his arms, bleeding all over his shirt. He was frightened. His eyes were huge, and he was white as a ghost. He should have been bright red from effort after hauling you across town."

"Awwww!" Josie murmured. "Well, I'm sure he was worried, as he would be with anyone who was bleeding profusely." She couldn't help it. She wanted to hear more about why Leigh thought Jefferson was attracted to her, but she didn't have the courage to prod Leigh any further. Jefferson was essentially a kind man, but he could not really have been interested in her in any romantic sense. Like Will, he was generally easygoing and lighthearted. She, ad nauseum, was not.

"I think it's more than that, Josie, but I won't harp on it. If I'm wrong, I don't want to get your hopes up."

Leigh gave her a sympathetic smile, hopefully not realizing that her words had sliced Josie just like a knife. In the space of two minutes, Josie had gone from incredulity to elation to skepticism to self-doubt to painful disappointment, and the subject of it all was Jefferson Lundrum.

"No hopes," Josie murmured. "None."

"Okay, that's good, I guess. Do you want to go now? I'll let Mrs. Jackson and Jeremiah know I'm leaving, and between them they can handle Jeri when she wakes up."

Josie nodded. "Yes, I guess we ought to."

"I think it's a great idea, Josie," Leigh said, rising. "Besides the excitement of opening your own business, a man is going to help you without asking anything in return. You really don't run into too many men like that, do you?"

Josie shrugged. Leigh really kept digging the pit. "I don't run into too many men at any rate, so I wouldn't know."

"Well, let's go," Leigh said.

They left the room and descended the stairs, where Leigh stopped by the kitchen to talk to Mrs. Jackson before going into the parlor to talk to Jeremiah in his office. Josie put her hat on, a little sailor hat with green ribbons, remembering that she must have left her other hat at Martha's boardinghouse. She tried to pin it on with her left hand but failed.

"Here, let me get that," Leigh said, emerging from the parlor to pin Josie's hat into her hair.

Jeremiah followed Leigh out, carrying a length of white cloth.

"Leigh tells me that you are going into town," he said. "We should put your arm in a sling. You do not need to dangle your hand about."

Josie stood still while Jeremiah fitted the sling over her shoulder and tied it at the back of her neck. Her hand throbbed, and she realized it had started sometime after Jefferson left.

"How does that feel?" he asked.

"Good, thanks."

"You do not need to wear it around the house, but if you are walking a distance, it would be better to keep your hand elevated to reduce swelling."

"I understand."

Leigh settled a sailor hat on her head and kissed Jeremiah's cheek before turning for the front door. She and Josie walked up Lakefront Lane toward town.

"What did Jeremiah say when you told him?" Josie asked.

"That I was going into town? He told me to enjoy myself."

"You didn't tell him that Jefferson was going to cosign a loan for me?"

"Not yet," Leigh said. "I'll let you tell him. I suppose you've heard that Will asked him for a loan to start a guide fishing business, and Jeremiah is going to loan him the money."

"I knew Will was going to ask him for a loan, and this morning Jeremiah asked me what he thought about Will's potential. I told him I didn't know Will that well but that he probably knew his fish."

Leigh chuckled.

"Why didn't you tell Jeremiah about Jefferson's offer?" Josie asked.

Leigh shrugged. "It's kind of your business really, and I didn't want to take the time. He had a patient in his office, and I wanted to touch base with him quickly. I didn't know he was going to come out and give you a sling. How does it feel?"

"Fine, thanks, probably better than swinging my hand around. I thought you didn't want to tell Jeremiah because you thought he might disapprove—either of my trying to start a business or signing a loan with Jefferson."

"No, not at all. Jeremiah wouldn't disapprove of either of those things. Honestly, he'd probably loan you the money if you wanted, since he's going to loan Will some."

"I wouldn't have asked," Josie said with a firm chin.

"I figured as much."

At the end of the road, they turned up toward town. Leigh nodded to passersby, the occasional person on horseback or driving a wagon.

"Do you know all those people?"

"No," Leigh said with a laugh. "It's just what they do here. It's not like in our day."

"No, I guess not."

They reached the commercial area and turned left onto the aptly named Main Street.

"Oh wait!" Josie exclaimed. "I wonder if this is the empty storefront that Jefferson said was available for rent."

Just two buildings down from the mercantile, a sign in the ground-floor large picture window of a two-story wooden building read "For Rent." Josie peered into the window. The store was empty of furnishings, shelving or anything that suggested what might have once been there. Dark paneling covered the walls, and two light globes hung from the ceiling.

"Well, it's square," Leigh said, peering in beside her. "So that's something."

"That's funny," Josie responded. "I can't laugh right now because of this knot in the pit of my stomach, but if that wasn't there, I would laugh."

"Yes, I'm sure you would," Leigh said.

"Where's the bathroom?" Josie asked.

"There's a door in the back. See it?"

"Oh, please say that doesn't lead to an outhouse," Josie muttered.

"I can't say that," Leigh said. She looked at Josie. "Do you want to see it before you apply for the loan?"

"I have the keys," Jefferson said from behind them. "I saw you from across the street and grabbed the keys, which I took the liberty of acquiring this morning. Would you like to look inside?"

"Yes, please," Josie replied.

Jefferson opened the door with a skeleton key and then stepped back to allow Josie and Leigh to precede him. Josie walked into the room and slapped a hand over her nose at the stench. Overlaying a musty smell of dust and mildew was an even fouler smell of human waste.

"That is terrible!" Jefferson said, though he didn't cover his mouth as both Josie and Leigh did.

"What is that?" Josie muttered, reluctant to move farther into the room.

"I'm going to guess there is a bathroom in here," Leigh said from behind her hand.

Jefferson strode to the door that they had seen earlier at the back of the store. He opened it, and the stench grew stronger.

"Shut it! I get it!" Josie said.

Jefferson shut the door. "That is a bathroom, and it needs to be cleaned. I cannot help but wonder if squatters have been in here. See where the dust has been disturbed?" He pointed to footprints other than his in the dust on the hardwood floor. "And there. Newspapers. Perhaps a place to sleep."

In the corner to the left of the window was a pile of newspapers that had been spread out.

"How did they get in?" Josie asked. "The front door was locked, wasn't it?"

"There is a door from the bathroom leading to an alley behind,"

Jefferson said. "I wonder if that was unlocked or pried open. I did not go through to check."

"Can we leave?" Josie said. Her body hummed with anxiety. She couldn't possibly spend time in the disgusting store, not even long enough to clean it. It wouldn't work. The whole bookstore thing wasn't going to work.

"I agree," Leigh said. "It's hard to think straight in here."

Jefferson escorted them to the door and locked it behind him.

"I am so sorry," he said with a rueful frown. "I had no idea. I must be sure and tell Mr. Hodges about the store. I am certain he will have it cleaned before leasing it out."

Josie shook her head. "I can't."

"It has good bones, Josie," Leigh said, taking in a deep breath as they stood on the boardwalk. "If the landlord gets it cleaned, it has great possibilities."

"I can't breathe," Josie responded, envying Leigh her big exhale.

"Here, let us put space between ourselves and the store and go over to my office," Jefferson said. "I am not aware of other available places in Kaskade, but we could certainly look. I thought this location eminently suitable, and its proximity to the mercantile certain to capture people in the frame of mind to spend money."

"Good thinking!" Leigh said with an enthusiasm that Josie couldn't share. Her dream of sweet-smelling colorful books had evaporated in a cloud of fumes and dust.

Leigh propelled Josie across the street toward a two-story building with a wooden false front. They entered the front door and stepped into an attractive foyer with a well-varnished wooden floor. A hallway led away toward open and closed doors, but Jefferson directed them up a staircase just across the foyer. They climbed the stairs to the second floor, where Jefferson opened one of many doors to allow them into his office.

Three windows let in a lovely amount of light, and Josie wasn't surprised to see that Jefferson's office was clean and tidy. A large wooden desk centered the room, with bookshelves lining several walls. Jefferson guided Josie and Leigh toward a chocolate-brown cloth sofa, and he seated himself in one of two matching easy chairs. The furnishings were stylishly simple and not at all ostentatious.

Through several of the windows, Josie could see the peaked roof of the mercantile.

"Is that how you saw us across the street?" she asked, pointing to the window.

Jefferson nodded. "Yes, I have a nice view of the business district." He hesitated, as if he wanted to think about his words.

Sitting in Jefferson's tidy office in his clean building, she felt awful at her outright rejection of the store.

"The store can be cleaned, Josie. You can hire someone to clean the store. In fact, you will have to, as I do not think your hand will have mended by then."

"By then?" Josie squeaked. "Wait! Is this happening right away? I'm not ready!"

"I believe someone else is interested in the store...or so Mr. Hodges said. That may just have been a ploy to galvanize me into action. He believes I am the interested party, as I did not wish to involve your name or purpose until I was certain you would like the place. But that must be your decision, Josie. I regret that I did not check the space before I let you in, or I could have requested that Mr. Hodges clean it. I am certain he cannot know what shape it is in."

"Well, besides the bathroom—which I didn't see—the store itself is in good shape," Leigh said. "It needs stuff—shelves, counters, books, coffee."

"Coffee?" Jefferson and Josie echoed.

Leigh laughed. "Just kidding. You know, Josie. Bookstores in our day often have coffee shops."

Josie nodded and relaxed. "Yes, that's true. The store would have to have plumbing to accommodate that—" She paused and wrinkled her nose. "Oh wait. It does have plumbing, kind of."

Jefferson grinned. "It does, and it shall be repaired. The rent is forty dollars a month. He requires a twelve-month lease, which would be just about correct for your stay."

"Is that all?" Josie gasped. She turned to Leigh. "I don't need a bank loan for that, do I?"

Leigh winced. "You do in 1910," she said. "That's actually quite a bit of money. I know, I know. It takes some getting used to."

Josie bit her lower lip and rose to cross over to the window. She looked down onto the mercantile, then let her eyes slide to the space for lease.

"A bookstore," she murmured. "I'm not sure I'd be very good with crunching numbers, especially without a computer."

"I can get you started, Josie," Leigh said. "I do Jeremiah's books. I'm terrible with math but pretty good at accounting. Go figure!"

"Have courage, Josie," Jefferson said. "There are many of us here who can help you with the business aspect of the store, but you are uniquely qualified to order the inventory and sell the product."

Josie turned and looked at Jefferson. The light filtered in through the window and highlighted his face as he smiled at her and nodded encouragement. Her hand stopped hurting, her heart expanded, and her ego swelled. Jefferson thought she could do it. She wanted to prove him right. She wanted to revel in the feeling that his approving smile gave her.

Chapter Thirteen

Jefferson saw the color rise in Josie's cheeks. Her chin lifted, and she nodded her head.

"Okay," she said. "I'm back on track. With your help, I'll rent the store on the condition that Mr. Hodges gets that place cleaned up. What's the next step? I promise I won't bother you with each and every detail once we get going, but for now, I don't even know where the bank is."

Jefferson rose. "The bank is just downstairs. The manager is an acquaintance of mine, and I already inquired about cosigning on a loan. Mr. Dunfield assured me that it is all very straightforward."

Leigh stood. "All righty then," she said. "I guess we're going to the bank."

The ladies moved to the door, and Jefferson followed them down the staircase. He wondered that he did not feel more uneasiness at entering a financial transaction with a virtual stranger, but he did not. The lease was only a year, and he truly believed it would not only make Josie happy but would also calm her nerves by giving her direction, tasks and accomplishments.

He could be mistaken, but he hoped for the best. She had been taken aback at the first misstep, and there might be more, but she had risen above it with encouragement and support.

The more he discovered about Josie, the more Jefferson wished he had offered his mother more encouragement, but he had been a young man full of himself and not inclined to offer his mother the support that his father failed to give.

He put his regrets aside and escorted Josie and Leigh into the bank, where the manager, Walter Dunfield, rose from a desk to greet them. Jefferson nodded toward the cashiers, two middle-aged men who looked up with curiosity.

"Jefferson," Walter said in a jovial tone. His paunch indicated that Mrs. Dunfield was an excellent cook. He nodded to Leigh and Josie. "Mrs. Cook. It is so nice to see you."

"Walter, this is Miss Josie Brookman. Miss Brookman and I are entering into a business together, and I would like to cosign a loan with her, as I discussed with you earlier."

"Miss Brookman! So nice to meet you. Please sit!" Walter indicated wooden armchairs in front of his desk.

The women sat.

"You did not say that you were cosigning for a *young lady*, Jefferson." Walter gave him a speculative look but kept his wide mustached smile. Sparse hair dotted the crown of his rounded face.

"No, I did not," Jefferson replied, keeping his own smile deliberately pleasant.

"So this will be a purely business arrangement?" Walter asked.

Jefferson turned quickly at the sound of Josie's gasp. Her cheeks were bright red, and she truly looked as if she might explode.

"Is there a problem with me being a *young lady*?" she asked.

Leigh put a hand over Josie's uninjured arm, a calming act for which Jefferson was grateful.

Walter blinked, apparently unused to such confrontation. Jefferson had to admit that even he was surprised at Josie's outburst.

"No!" Walter exclaimed. "You appear to be a very attractive young woman, but we do not loan money to young unmarried ladies as a rule. Surely you must know that. If you and Jefferson were to be wed, then I could see the logic in loaning you the money. I am simply inquiring—"

"Wed? No!" Josie interrupted. "We're not getting married. What is this about? Do I have to be married to get a loan?" Josie's body visibly shook.

"Well, yes, Miss Brookman," Walter said. "I think you must know that is why Jefferson has consented to cosign a loan with you. How can the bank reasonably collect on you should you default on the loan?"

Jefferson wondered if it would be helpful if he were to put another restraining hand on Josie's other arm.

"By taking the business for which I'm taking the loan!" she hissed through trembling lips.

"Josie," Jefferson entreated. He did not know what sort of business practices she was accustomed to, but they must certainly have been different. He could not at that moment remind her of such.

"But just think how well the business will be doing by next year in *1911*, Josie," Leigh said. "You'll have the loan paid back in no time at all."

Josie blinked and looked at Leigh. Her mouth worked, and her visible shaking eased. Suddenly, her shoulders slumped, and she turned back to Walter, who had been throwing alarmed looks toward Jefferson.

"Yes, I see what you mean," Josie said docilely. "I really appreciate that Mr. Lundrum is willing to cosign the loan. He's going to be a silent partner in the business."

Walter blinked at Josie's sudden change in demeanor, and he looked at Jefferson for reassurance.

Jefferson nodded, as if everything were perfectly normal. "Yes, that is true."

"Very well," Walter said. "Let us draw up the papers." He called Roger, one of the cashiers, over, and they set the loan in motion. Walter seemed to realize they were still sitting there, and he looked up.

"If you could return in about two hours, we could have the funds available for you."

"Very good," Jefferson said. "We will return."

Jefferson rose and escorted the women out of the bank, stepping away from the door and pausing on the boardwalk.

"We should visit Mr. Hodges and let him know that you intend to take the store," he said, studying Josie's pinched face. He looked uncertainly at Leigh.

"We don't have to rely on men to get loans anymore, Jefferson," Leigh whispered, because of the presence of passersby. "Josie's just stunned at the moment. She got the typical 'don't worry your pretty head about that' treatment."

Josie's pinched face relaxed, and she looked up at Jefferson. "I'm sorry. I could have handled that better. Leigh is right. I was shocked. Thank you for the calendar reminder," she said to Leigh, a smile curving her lips. "Very subtle. Nice touch!"

Leigh inclined her head with a chuckle. "I know, right? I thought it was pretty good."

"I did not know what to say," Jefferson murmured. "I suspected business dealings might be different in your time, but I could not broach the subject at that time."

"I'll do better," Josie said with a firm nod. "Bring on this Mr. Hodges. I'm all over that guy. Kid gloves. Obsequious. A 'young lady.' I defer to you, Mr. Lundrum, in all things."

Her smile took the sting from her words, though he had no idea what "I'm all over that guy" meant. It sounded odd, somewhat violent. He did not want to ask. He discovered that he had developed a soft spot for Josie, a tenderness for her idiosyncratic character that made him want to protect her. To his surprise, he ran not *from* her complicated nature but toward it. He, who had always preferred uncomplicated, cheerful women—or so he thought.

He shook his head, as if to dismiss his aberrant thoughts.

"Hello again!" Belinda called out, approaching them on the boardwalk.

As if he had conjured an uncomplicated, cheerful woman, she appeared. Though truth be told, Belinda had an adventurous spirit that Jefferson did not share. He loved Kaskade. Belinda did not.

Collin walked beside her.

"Oh, Belinda! Collin," Leigh said as they came to stand beside them. "I'm so very sorry about last night. As my note said, we had an emergency, and we had to call dinner off."

Jefferson turned to look at Josie. Had it only been yesterday? What had he been thinking carrying her all over town with her recent blood loss?

He noted that she looked from him to Belinda with a curious expression.

"We understand fully, do we not, Collin? I do hope everything is all right. Goodness, Josie! What happened? Were you the emergency?"

"What happened to you, poor girl?" Collin asked.

Josie's face reddened.

Certain that she did not want to be the center of attention, Jefferson spoke for her. "Yes, Josie cut herself, but she is on the mend. Are you and Collin shopping today?"

Belinda smiled brightly. "In a manner of speaking. We just finished visiting with Mr. Hodges. Collin and I plan to purchase a house."

"Congratulations!" Jefferson said. Josie and Leigh echoed his words. "Then you plan to stay in Kaskade?"

"The hotel has become far too expensive for my taste," Collin added. "I have convinced Belinda to settle in Kaskade until at least next summer."

Any mention of summer always sent certain eyebrows up, and Collin's mention was no exception. He was not one of the few people who knew about the time travelers...as far as Jefferson knew.

"That is good news," Jefferson said automatically. He remembered Belinda as a very lovely girl and would have welcomed the idea that she was moving back to town, except at that moment, his concern was for Josie, whose face was pale once again.

"I think we must leave you now," Jefferson said, knowing his comment was abrupt and without good reason. The plan to open a bookstore was not his to share.

"Good day, Belinda! Collin," he said, ushering Josie and Leigh past the couple as they said a bewildered goodbye. Jefferson suspected the siblings would follow their progress into Mr. Hodges' office, from which they had just come. Mr. Hodges owned the only realty business in town, and in doing so, he owned most of the properties available for lease and sale.

They moved down the boardwalk, and Jefferson stopped in front of a door over which the sign "Hodges Realty" hung. He reached for the door handle just as the door swung open to reveal a small mouse of a man in an oversized brown suit and bespectacled eyes. Thin strands of black hair combed over his scalp mirrored an equally sparse mustache.

"Mr. Lundrum!" Stanley Hodges crowed, stepping back to allow them to enter his office. "Have you seen the place yet? What did you think?"

"Mr. Hodges, allow me to introduce Miss Josie Brookman. You know Mrs. Cook, I presume?"

"Mrs. Cook! How is the good doctor? I really must make my annual visit."

"He's well, Mr. Hodges. It is nice to see you," Leigh said, her tone professionally pleasant.

Jefferson sensed that she did not care for Hodges very much.

"Miss Brookman, my pleasure," Mr. Hodges said, taking her hand and bowing over it in a chivalrous manner that seemed far too effusive to suit Jefferson's tastes.

Josie withdrew her hand quickly. "It's nice to meet you, Mr. Hodges."

"Please, please, take a seat!" Hodges moved to pull another wooden armchair up in front of his desk, where two already sat in place.

The furnishings in his office were ornate, suggesting he did very well in real estate. A ruby-red carpet covered the floor, and the oak desk was as oversized as he was small. Gilt-framed landscapes more suited to a stately dining room than a realty office covered the walls.

"Thank you," Jefferson said. He looked at Josie, wondering if he should defer to her to speak, but she nodded at him, and he understood he must handle the negotiations. He was grateful that she conceded such, for Hodges was known to be a wily character.

Jefferson withdrew the key from his pocket and laid it on the counter.

"I am sorry, Mr. Hodges, but the store is a foul mess. I cannot rent it."

Josie gasped and turned to Jefferson, but he kept his gaze steadily on the realty agent.

"Whatever can you mean, Mr. Lundrum?"

"The bathroom is most foul. I cannot imagine what happened in there, but it does appear as if tramps have been staying in your store. Perhaps the door leading from the bathroom is unlocked. I could not stay long enough to discover. Do you have any other suitable properties for a store? Something here in the business district?"

"I cannot imagine what has happened! How can I remedy this? The building is sound, the walls of the store in good shape. What can I do to convince you to lease the property?"

"The bathroom would need to be completely replaced, perhaps modernized with the latest fixtures and plumbing. Of course, the entire store must be cleaned at your expense. The tramps have left debris on the floor. I think in order to accept a lease for a place in this condition, I might accept a reduction in the rent by fifteen percent a month...in addition to the renovation of the bathroom and cleaning. Otherwise, do you have any other properties you would like to show me?"

"Nothing commercial," he said, his small shoulders slumping. "I have several offices and some homes, but I suspect none of those will do for a bookstore, as you have suggested."

"No, they will not." Jefferson was aware of Josie's efforts to conceal a smile as she raised her uninjured hand to her mouth. So attuned had he become to her that he thought she held her breath as she awaited Hodges' response.

"Very well then, Mr. Lundrum. We are in a bit of a realty slump, or I would not consider your proposal. I will assess the bathroom, renovate it—"

"With the most modern fixtures," Jefferson inserted.

"With the most modern fixtures. I will have the store cleaned, secure whatever entrance was used, and I will reduce the rent by fifteen percent. In return, I would like a minimum of a two-year lease for my efforts—quid pro quo."

Jefferson pressed his lips together. He cast a sideways glance at Josie, who threw him a startled look.

"You have my assurance that I will lease the store for two years. That is acceptable to me. When can I expect the repairs to be complete?"

Hodges thought for a moment. "I imagine I can have the work done in three weeks. Would that be satisfactory?"

Jefferson looked at Josie, who lifted her sling and nodded.

"Yes, that would be quite nice. Thank you."

Jefferson could not help but preen a bit. For some reason, he wished to champion Josie, and he thought he had done very well that morning.

"I will deliver one year's rent to you in several hours," he said. "Perhaps I should have mentioned that Miss Brookman will be signing the lease and providing the funds. I am certain that is of no consequence to you. I know you have only just met Miss Brookman, but I can vouch for her.”

“Mr. Lundrum!” Mr. Hodges protested. “What is the meaning of this? You have not negotiated fairly!”

“I believe I have, Mr. Hodges. As I said, I have vouched for Miss Brookman. We will deliver an entire year of rent to you. What else could you require?”

Out of the corner of his eye, Jefferson noted Josie’s lips moving, as if she spoke to herself. He thought he recognized the word “obsequious.”

“I will require that you also sign the lease.”

“This is Miss Brookman’s store. I do not think that is necessary.”

“No, that’s fine, Jefferson,” Josie said. “Mr. Lundrum is my silent partner, so I don’t mind if he signs the lease. Thank you for cleaning and renovating the place, Mr. Hodges. I look forward to seeing the most modern fixtures for the bathroom. It was nice of you to agree to that. I will make sure the customers know what a good landlord you are.”

Mr. Hodges’ cheeks turned red, and he looked at Josie as if he could not tell if she was serious.

She bared her teeth at him in a vacuous smile, and he nodded.

“Very well. I look forward to doing business with you,” he said.

Jefferson rose and helped Josie up. Leigh stood at the same time as Hodges. He escorted them to the door a little less enthusiastically than when he’d greeted them.

Once outside, Josie could not hold back a laugh. “Jefferson!” she exclaimed. “You could have told us! I thought you were just canceling the whole deal. And then I wasn’t quite sure what I was going to do if he called your bluff.”

“A modern bathroom, Josie!” Leigh exclaimed. “That’s a huge concession. Nice going, Jefferson!”

“Thank you!” Josie said, equally enthusiastic.

Jefferson’s cheeks warmed, and he pulled his shoulders back at the appreciative look in Josie’s eyes. If he had to describe the feeling, he thought he positively basked.

He shook his head.

"Just a bit of maneuvering. I had no doubt that he would come around. You acquitted yourself quite well in there. Did I see you mouthing the word 'obsequious'?"

"Over and over," Josie said with a grin.

"I have to get back to the house," Leigh said. "Jeri will be up and wanting her mother. Can I leave Josie with you, Jefferson? You have to go back to the bank in about an hour and a half, right?"

Jefferson noted Josie stiffen. Her smile faded. Disappointment hit him hard in the stomach. Surely she could manage an hour or so in his company. He did not think she disliked him. Was she afraid of him? Surely not! Uneasy? Why? He thought he must take the opportunity to ask. Ironically, the idea of asking Josie how she felt about him made him uneasy.

Jefferson nodded in response to Leigh but waited for Josie's reaction.

"Okay," she said quietly.

He supposed her flat response was better than an outright refusal to stay. "We could have lunch in the café, if you like?" he asked.

"That's a good idea," Leigh voiced. "Okay, I have to go. You'll see her home, won't you, Jefferson?"

"Yes, of course."

"Bye," Josie said.

Jefferson hoped he didn't hear a wistful note in her voice but thought he did. Leigh hurried away down the boardwalk, leaving Josie and Jefferson standing together in awkward silence, she looking down at her feet.

Jefferson wanted to lift her chin to force her to look at him, but he dared not.

"Josie," he said softly, as if speaking to a shy colt.

"Yes?"

"Is something wrong?"

"No," she murmured. "It's just—"

She kept her head down, and he could not lean over enough to see her expression.

"I thought we were on more comfortable footing this morning. Was I wrong?"

"No, I felt fine this morning."

"What has changed?"

"Well, I'm not sure this was your idea—me hanging out here. I don't think Leigh gave you any choice. You probably have stuff to do, and I'm not really sure I can entertain you for a whole hour and a half, and I wouldn't know what to talk about, and I'm really sure you have other stuff to do. I could come back!" She finally lifted her head to look at him.

Jefferson almost laughed. Almost. But he could not at the intensity in Josie's eyes. Worry darkened their color to a mixed shade of forest green.

"Josie, Josie," he said, picking up her uninjured hand and bringing it to his lips in an old-fashioned gesture. "I have nothing better to do than have lunch with you. Do not fret. You have no need to set yourself to 'entertain me.' Your company is entertainment enough. That is *not* to say that I find you laughable, but I am often amused by you. I hope that you take my words as a compliment."

He tucked her hand under his arm. "Shall we have lunch?"

Josie nodded and then proceeded to crumple. He caught her around the waist again as she fainted.

CHAPTER FOURTEEN

Josie opened her eyes to a face close to hers. Familiar blue eyes peered into hers.

"Josie?" Jefferson prompted.

"What happened?" she asked, finding herself half-prone on the boardwalk, the upper half of her body cradled in his arms as he kneeled.

"I believe you fainted. I need to carry you home to Jeremiah."

"No! No, I'm fine," she said, trying to sit upright. Curious faces stared at them, and she heard the occasional question about her welfare.

"Poor girl. Is she well?" the female half of a couple passing by asked.

"Yes, she slipped. She is fine," Jefferson replied.

"I don't think I slipped," Josie whispered when they moved on.

"No, you fainted, as you did yesterday. I suspect today has been too arduous for you. That is my fault for pressing you to see the store, go to the bank and to the realty office. No, really, it has all been too much! What was I thinking?"

"You were thinking you wanted to help me, and I appreciate that. While you're at it, I could use your help getting up."

Jefferson helped Josie stand, and she leaned against him for a moment to steady herself. He kept his arms around her. She looked down at her sling, which seemed intact. Her hand didn't hurt. It never seemed to hurt when she was around Jefferson.

"I caught you before you fell," he said, following her gaze.

"How long was I out?"

"Seconds really. Not long at all, but I am truly concerned about you."

Josie bit her lip. "Don't be, Jefferson. I should probably confess. I've passed out before."

"Yes, yesterday when you had lost blood."

"I doubt if it was the blood loss yesterday either."

"How can you know that?"

"Because like I said, I've fainted before. About four or five times in my life."

"Have you seen a doctor for your condition? Did you mention as much to Jeremiah? He could have examined you for that. He could send you to Tacoma to be examined for fainting spells."

"No need. I had an examination last year. My heart is fine. My blood pressure is fine. It's the anxiety. I tend to hold my breath and don't realize I'm doing it. Then I get woozy, and sometimes I faint."

"You hold your breath?"

Josie nodded. "When I get nervous."

"What made you so anxious just now that you held your breath?"

"Oh dear, you're going to think I'm a nitwit."

"I would *never* think you were such a thing."

"I was worried about having lunch with you, what to say or do. I have a feeling that you're impatient with anxious people, and worrying about that only stresses me out even more."

A lump formed in Jefferson's throat, and he lowered his eyes to the ground. "Please forgive me," he muttered. "I did not mean to cause you worry. You are not incorrect. I have been somewhat impatient with fretful people. My mother was one such, and she was difficult—" He cut short his words.

"To live with?" Josie offered. "I can imagine."

"That is not what I was about to say, Josie. I was about to say she was difficult to understand, to predict. As you mention it now, I do believe that she fainted on several occasions as well. We always called her swooning spells 'the vapors,' but that term is not in use today. I think it was derisive on our part, and I regret its use and the condemnation we associated with it. Not Martha, never Martha, who was a loving daughter, but my father and I. I truly do regret it, but it is too late to make amends."

"You said we were similar. She sounds a *lot* like me actually."

"In some ways, yes. You look nothing like her, but you do share a few similarities."

"I'm okay now," Josie said, noting people still staring at them curiously as they passed, maybe because she still leaned against his tall, secure body. She took a step away. "Should we go eat? Maybe that's what I need."

"If you feel up to it, certainly." He held out his arm, and she took it. They crossed the street and walked toward a nondescript one-story wood building. Josie saw the chimney stack billowing and smelled food as they approached.

They stepped inside, and Josie was pleasantly surprised to see that it resembled any number of small neighborhood cafés in the twenty-first century. Checked tablecloths covered small square four-person tables. Two waitresses in aprons took orders.

Josie and Jefferson were seated at a table in a back corner and handed menus.

Josie's eyes widened at the prices.

"Five cents for soup? Really? Oh, I'm going to like living here." She bit her lip, and her heart started beating fast. "Except...I don't have any cash. I'm sorry. Do you mind buying? I know that's rude to ask."

"Not at all, Josie. I invited you, so it is natural that I should pay. Additionally, you are a lady, so it is natural that I should pay."

"Oh boy, you really are old fashioned," Josie said with a relieved smile.

"Am I?"

She nodded.

The waitress appeared, not in a short pink uniform but in a white cotton shirtwaist and long serviceable gray serge skirt covered by a full-length apron.

"What would you like to order?" she asked.

"Good day, Mrs. Broward," Jefferson said, obviously no stranger to the café. He introduced Josie as a newcomer, and then they ordered.

"Everything is cooked all the way through, right?" Josie leaned in to ask in a whisper after Mrs. Broward left. "I hate to be so fussy, but I can't help it."

"Yes, I am certain the tomato soup is cooked all the way through." Jefferson looked more amused than irritated, and Josie took that as a good sign.

"Sorry. I don't mean to be obnoxious."

"You are not obnoxious."

"And they wash the vegetables, right? The tomatoes? To get rid of pesticides?"

"Ah! Insecticides! Why do you ask about that?"

"They're terrible for you!" Josie whispered urgently. "Well, for human consumption."

"And you believe washing the produce is necessary?"

"I'll bet Jeremiah does. I noticed Mrs. Jackson washes all the food. I'm sure Leigh had something to do with that."

"But still the soup is cooked. Would it not evaporate?"

"I don't know!" Josie's stomach rolled over. "And I'm starving."

"We will ask Mrs. Broward when she returns, as her daughter does most of the cooking. It is that simple."

"You can't! What if they think it's a weird question, like something someone from the future would ask?"

"I cannot imagine that they would even imagine such a thing."

Out of the corner of her eye, Josie saw Mrs. Broward returning with a basket of bread. Josie tried to signal Jefferson not to ask the question, but he did.

"Mrs. Broward, I would like to ask a question, if you do not mind."

"Certainly, Mr. Lundrum."

"I recently read a report of arsenic poisoning in apples. I do not know if you read it. But it made me wonder. Do we wash our fruits and vegetables enough? I mentioned the article to Martha, and she immediately started washing all her foodstuffs. Have you heard anything about that in the restaurant industry?"

"We did read about that, Mr. Lundrum, though that was over ten years ago. We wash everything. I wish I could chat more, but it is our busy hour. Your soup will be here soon."

She hurried away, and Jefferson dropped his eyes to Josie, a grin plastered across his face.

"Thank you for asking!" she said, responding to his self-satisfied smile. "Now go tell Martha to wash her vegetables, especially the potatoes!" With a half smile, Josie lifted her hand.

"She already does, as you know. I did actually read that newspaper article in the past and passed the information on to Martha. I had forgotten until you used the word *pesticides*."

"Tell me more about your mother," Josie said.

"What would you like to know?"

"You said she wasn't always a nervous sort of person?"

Jefferson shook his head. "No, not when she was younger, when we were small children."

"I always have been," Josie said. "I wonder what made your mother anxious? How she became that way?"

Jefferson had given that some thought, but he could not choose an event, a single year, or even a period of several years when she changed. He shook his head.

"Martha might have a better idea. She was closer to our mother."

"I understand," Josie said. "It's probably none of my business anyway. Maybe I feel a kinship with her, since I remind you of her."

"She would like that, Josie. She was a lonely woman. I remember that now as well. I probably did not realize it at the time. She may very well have enjoyed knowing you."

To her surprise, Josie's eyes teared up, and she wiped at them with a tremulous smile.

"What was her name?"

"Joanna Lundrum," he said. "She emigrated from Norway with my father."

"You're kidding! That's my name!" Josie cried out.

"What do you mean?" Jefferson asked.

"Joanna! That's my name! For some reason, my parents just called me Josie, and it stuck. How coincidental is that!"

"Very coincidental," Jefferson said with a smile.

"No wonder I feel a kinship with her," Josie said.

Mrs. Broward arrived with their orders. Jefferson had followed Josie's lead and ordered the tomato soup as well.

"This is delicious!" Josie said.

Jefferson agreed. "And washed!"

She chuckled. "You'll thank me one day!" she said with a wag of her finger.

"I already do."

His lips curved even further in what she could only describe as a tender smile. She caught her breath and dropped her eyes to her food. Her heart jumped around, and her hand shook as she spooned her soup into a tumultuous stomach.

Josie avoided direct eye contact with Jefferson for the rest of the meal. She didn't like the feelings his gaze was invoking in her. Her stomach spasmed, her body ran hot then cold, and her hair stood on end. She realized that she had become infatuated with him, but did it have to feel so tumultuous, so out of control? Couldn't she just like him in a calm, stress-free fashion? Couldn't she just shoot him the occasional smile, make a whimsical joke or flirtatiously glance up at him from under her eyelashes? Instead, she wondered where the nearest bathroom was, breathing deeply and hoping the sensation passed.

"You did not eat much," Jefferson said after a period of silence.

Josie had thought she was fooling him by repeatedly dipping the tip of her spoon and settling a drop of soup on her tongue.

"Oh sure I did," she said, looking down at the almost full bowl.

"Are you well? You look pale."

"I'm fine," she said, keeping her eyes on the soup. "Just fine. We should probably get back to the bank. It's close enough to two hours, isn't it?"

"Yes, I believe so. Are you certain you're quite well, Josie? You can tell me if you are not. I am concerned about you." His voice practically purred.

"No need to worry about me," Josie said, gritting her teeth against another stomach spasm. "We should hurry."

Out of the corner of her eye, Josie saw Jefferson raise a finger as if to catch Mrs. Broward's attention. She assumed he was getting the check. When the waitress arrived, Jefferson leaned up and spoke in a quiet tone, necessitating that Mrs. Broward bend to hear his words. She nodded and pointed somewhere.

When she left, Jefferson rose and approached Josie's chair. He took her unharmed arm and helped her up from her seat.

"Thank you," she said. "We didn't pay the bill. Do you have a tab or something?"

"I am not leaving just yet. I am going to escort you to the rear of the restaurant, however."

"What? Why?" Josie mumbled, following along as he guided her past a few tables and down a short hall near the kitchen. He stopped in front of a door.

"I have seen that look on your face before, Josie," he said with a gentle smile. "I will await you at the table."

With that, he pushed the door to the bathroom open for her.

CHAPTER FIFTEEN

Three weeks later, on his way to the office, Jefferson noted that the door to the store stood open. He had only seen Josie on two occasions in the intervening weeks since they had signed the loan and delivered the rent to Mr. Hodges. On both occasions when he had stopped by the Cook house to inquire about her welfare, he had seen her in Leigh's company in the parlor. Josie had responded to questions monosyllabically and avoided his gaze.

Jefferson wondered at her coldness, as he had imagined they had become friends, or at the very least amiable business partners. Had he assumed more to their arrangement than was there? Did she feel he had presumed on their business arrangement?

Unable to speak to Josie freely in private on the matter, he had taken what he believed to be her unspoken discomfort in his presence and had left her alone. Never did he wish her to believe that she owed him for his assistance. Never! And yet he suspected that was what concerned her.

He crossed the street and approached the open doorway of the store, stopping at the entrance. Knocking on the wooden sill, he called out. "Hello there! Is anyone here?"

Over the past three weeks, he had discreetly monitored the renovations Mr. Hodges had made to the place, but he had not wanted Josie to know that he kept an eye on the project.

The store looked immaculately swept and dusted but very, very empty. The door to the renovated restroom was closed, and Jefferson hesitated, wondering if he should leave. Perhaps it was not Josie in the bathroom but Mr. Hodges. Yes, that was more likely.

"Mr. Hodges, is that you?" Jefferson called out.

The bathroom door opened, and Josie emerged. Startlingly lovely in a lavender blouse and purple skirt, she patted at a black sailor hat before looking up to see him. Her bandage had been removed, and her hand appeared to be in good condition.

"Jefferson!" she cried out.

"Good morning, Josie. I apologize for barging in. The door was open. I thought you might be Mr. Hodges...or you, actually. I hoped to see you."

Josie placed a hand on her stomach and looked over her shoulder toward the bathroom.

"Are you ill?" Jefferson asked.

"Please stop asking me that all the time. Yes! I'm nervous, my stomach hurts, and I'm stressed out! The bathroom is all done. It's beautiful, I'm going to need it in the future, but now nothing is coming between me and the arrival of books today."

"Books! Arriving today? Where will you put them? You will need shelves, will you not?"

"Leigh's cousin's husband is delivering them today as well. He built a bunch of them, and he's bringing them down from Orting on a wagon."

"Ah! That must be William Ferguson. I met him. Very nice man. You have certainly been industrious since the last time I saw you."

"Oh, no, we've been working on this since I first got the keys. I didn't mention it to you when you visited because..."

She did not finish her sentence, and Jefferson wished to know the answer. Yet he was afraid of the answer. He supposed he must speak now.

"Josie, if you feel that I have forced myself on you in any way, if you feel that I have imposed upon our business arrangement in an inappropriate fashion, please say so at once. You owe me nothing. There is no commitment on your part to me, and I hope that I have not appeared to require anything from you...including your company."

Josie stared at him open mouthed, then dropped her head to stare at the floor. Jefferson felt he had indeed hit the mark. Her next words confirmed as much.

"I'm sorry, Jefferson, but—"

Jefferson interrupted. "Forgive me. It was never my intention to impose upon you. I wish you the best of luck." His throat knotted, and he quickly doffed his hat before turning and leaving. He strode across the street in a cloud of dust and took the stairs to his office two at a time. Upon reaching his office, he fumbled for his keys with a shaking hand, requiring him to use both hands to steady the key in the lock.

Collin, on his way out of his office, stopped short. Jefferson did not wish to speak to anyone.

"Is everything all right, Jefferson?" he asked.

"Everything is fine, thank you. These keys are difficult to manage."

"Yes, I agree. How have you been? I noted that Miss Brookman is opening a bookstore across the way. Brava to her! She is very enthusiastic about her project. She said she is to have bookshelves delivered today."

Jefferson's shoulders slumped, and he turned around.

"You know a great deal," he said morosely.

"She is a very nice young lady. I did wonder how she will manage the store and whether that is something Belinda might do."

"Open a bookstore?" Jefferson muttered.

"No, of course not, but an art gallery. Perhaps that is too ambitious for Kaskade."

"I could not say."

"Is everything all right, Jefferson? You sound very gloomy. It is not like you."

"I am gloomy," Jefferson finally admitted. "But I will soon cheer up."

"Is there anything I can do? I will not be in the office today, but if there is anything I can do, please let me know."

"Thank you. There is nothing. As I said, it will pass."

Collin nodded, and Jefferson turned back to struggle with his key. To his surprise, Collin appeared at his side, taking the key from him. He easily inserted the key and opened the door.

"You are fond of Miss Brookman, are you not?" Collin asked, handing Jefferson his key. "I saw that you were when we met weeks ago, and I mentioned as much to Belinda. She said she saw it as well."

Jefferson felt too glum to prevaricate or even to tell Collin to mind his own business.

"Yes, but I fear my affections are not returned."

"Women are such strange creatures, are they not?" Collin asked.

"Indeed they are," Jefferson said.

"Miss Brookman told me that you helped her acquire the store. That was kind of you."

"She mentioned me to you?"

"Yes. She volunteered that information. I certainly did not ask."

"It was nothing," Jefferson said. "Strictly a business arrangement."

"I suspect your assistance means a great deal to her. Have heart."

Jefferson did not have heart. He wanted only to bury himself in his work.

"Good day, Collin."

"And to you as well." Collin turned and left.

Jefferson opened the door, and his eyes went immediately to the windows overlooking the street...and Josie's store. A small part of him wondered what she intended to name the store as he pulled the blinds down. He turned and surveyed his office—a benign place where he had once busied himself with work but that had turned lonely and barren over the past few weeks.

He hung up his coat and jacket before settling down at his desk to attend to some paperwork. Though the blinds had been closed, he could still hear sounds from the business district coming through the windows. Wheels of wagons creaked, horses plodded and neighed, an occasional voice called out.

He could not keep his attention on his work, but he dared not look out the window. Josie might look up and see him, perhaps assume that he watched her.

For an hour he stared at paperwork, doing little else other than read and reread the words over again. When he could stand it no longer, he rose and approached one of the windows. He touched the blinds with his fingertips, then turned his back to the window.

He paced across the floor before returning to his chair behind the desk. Once again, he forced himself to attend to his work. Another hour passed, and he found that he had done nothing. Still the sounds outside the window compelled him. He could not resist. He jumped up again and approached the window.

Perhaps if he just stood to the side, he could peer out the crack between the blind and the window.

A knock on the door startled him, and he jumped back, as if he had been caught. He strode to the door, almost grateful for the distraction of a client.

Josie stood there, a basket in her hands.

"I come bearing gifts," she said with a tremulous smile.

Jefferson's own smile was unsteady. He stared at her as if he had seen a ghost.

"Peace offering?" she asked, holding up the basket with effort.

Jefferson stepped back, then stepped forward and took the basket from her. It was indeed heavy.

"Come in! Come in!" he said. "Forgive my staring. I am surprised to see you."

He escorted her to one of the chairs in front of his desk. He set the basket on the edge of the desk and turned.

"I imagine you probably are," Josie said with a rueful smile. "You didn't let me finish before you stormed off."

Jefferson leaned on his desk, hoping he appeared more calm than he felt.

"I did *not* 'storm off.' I imagined I strode off."

"Okay, strode off then."

"I apologize. There is no excuse for such behavior."

"I brought you an early lunch," Josie said.

Jefferson had almost forgotten the basket. He turned to it. "You did?"

Josie rose and came to stand beside him, so close he thought he could smell roses...perhaps her soap? She opened the basket and retrieved a white ceramic bowl covered in a cloth. Jefferson recognized the dishware as belonging to the café. Removing the cloth, Josie revealed a bowl of tomato soup. She set the soup on the desk and pulled out some bread and a spoon.

"This is wonderful!" he exclaimed. "Thank you. Where is your soup?"

Josie put a hand to her stomach before dropping it. "Oh, I'm not hungry. William is across the street installing the shelving, so I thought I'd get you some lunch and hope that you weren't too upset with me."

"Never!" Jefferson replied. "I could never be upset with you, Josie."

Her cheeks turned rosy. "I'll hold you to that."

"Why are you not hungry though? Are you still concerned about eating food that has not been washed?"

Josie shook her head. "No, I believe they wash their food. I'm just not hungry. That's all."

"Such a shame," he said. "There is more than enough for two people."

Josie turned away. "Well, I'd better get back and see how things are going. I'm not really needed there, but I'm pretty excited about how things are going, so I want to get back."

"May I look in later? Would that bother you?"

"Why would that bother me, Jefferson? I'm not really sure what you were talking about earlier, but you haven't 'imposed' on me or whatever it was you were talking about. Of course you can come look at the progress."

She turned toward the door, and he stopped himself from begging her to stay. "Josie!" he called out.

She turned at the door. He approached her but resisted taking her hands, though he wanted more than anything to do so.

"For the past three weeks, I have had the distinct impression that the sight of me was making you ill. Was I mistaken?"

Josie looked up at him with her beautiful almond-shaped hazel eyes.

"No, you weren't mistaken, Jefferson. You *are* making me ill."

He drew in a sharp breath at her unexpected response. She pulled open the door and looked over her shoulder before passing through. "But I'll get over it. I'm going to have to!"

With that, she shut the door behind her, leaving him more confused than before.

He resisted the urge to open the door and clatter down the stairs after her, requesting clarification on her comment, choosing instead to walk toward the window and lift the shade. She emerged from the building, glanced up over her shoulder then crossed the street. A wagon stood in front of her shop, and William Ferguson emerged from the store to retrieve one of many bookshelves. Jefferson marveled that the older man could carry such a heavy object over his shoulder, but he did.

Jefferson looked over his shoulder toward his desk and the work that awaited him. The basket Josie had thoughtfully brought by awaited him as well. But what he truly wanted to do was go across the street and help William carry in the bookshelves, and ultimately help Josie set up her store. He wanted to be involved in her project. He wanted to become involved with *her*.

Jefferson watched her walk into her shop. He admitted to himself that he had missed her over the past three weeks. His visits to the Cook house had been emotionally sterile, and he had not wanted to acknowledge that they had been hurtful.

The door to the store was empty of activity, yet Jefferson continued to stare at it, wondering when he had fallen in love...and how. Did Kaskade truly have the power to bring people together? Was he to be one more statistic in Kaskade's history of matchmaking across the centuries? Unless he fought his heart's desire, then yes, it was true. He was to be one more statistic, for he was in love with the time traveler he had found.

William emerged from the store and climbed into the back of the wagon to position another shelf for removal. Even from that distance, Jefferson could see that his back ached, as he straightened gingerly before climbing down.

Jefferson would have thought nothing of helping an older man carry a heavy object, but he feared Josie would see it as interference in her store. She had clearly not wished to discuss her progress with him when she had ordered shelving and books. It appeared that they were not even to be silent partners as they had discussed. Perhaps that description of their relationship had only been said to facilitate the loan. It had never been his intention to oversee her project, but only to help her find happiness during her year in Kaskade.

He watched William maneuver the next shelf from the wagon with more difficulty than previously.

A year. One year was all he would have of Josie, even as a largely business transaction. No, not a year. Eleven months. Eleven months would pass as if they were days. There was no time to waste.

He left the office and ran down the stairs to cross the road.

"William, how nice to see you!" he called out as he approached. "Can I help you?"

William, a tall, slender man with a thick handlebar mustache, turned to him with an expression of relief.

"I remember you. Jefferson, right?"

Jefferson offered his hand. "Yes, Jefferson Lundrum. I am acquainted with Miss Brookman, and I was watching you, from my office across the street, carry in shelves. If we form a team, we could carry the rest of the shelves inside in minimum time."

"I would be so grateful," William said, the corners of his mustache lifting in a rueful smile. "I don't mind building things, but I'm getting a bit long in the tooth for hauling them around. I couldn't rustle up any young helpers today, and I promised to deliver the shelves today."

"I am happy to help."

Together they lifted one shelf and carried it into the store. Josie, bent over a wooden box, straightened to direct the position of the shelf.

"Jefferson!" she exclaimed, startled to see him there, as he knew she would be. "That's nice of you to help William."

Jefferson could not help but preen a little at the appreciative note in her voice. He found himself craving her approval.

"Not at all," he said. "I thought it might go faster if I helped."

"I'm glad he is helping," William said. "Ready for another?"

"Indeed," Jefferson said. Out of the corner of his eye, he surveyed Josie, who had dropped her eyes to a stack of books in her hand. She looked well enough, not at all ill in his presence. He had to know more about that.

Chapter Sixteen

Two weeks later, Josie opened her doors for business, with Leigh at her side. As she pushed open the door, she looked up at Jefferson's office window across the street, wondering if he could see her.

Her heart soared as he pulled open the window and bent down to grin at her.

"Congratulations!" he called out over the sound of a wagon lumbering by in the road.

"Thank you!" she called out with a wave.

Leigh came to stand by her side. She too waved at Jefferson, who responded before closing his window against the dust kicking up from the wagon.

"Well, here you go!" Leigh said as they retreated into the store. "Remember now, I need receipts for everything! And do your best to remember that five cents is a lot of money!"

Josie laughed. She had studied the money carefully, and Leigh had her practice purchasing a few things in the mercantile to get a feel of the value of money in 1910.

"Everything looks so nice!" Leigh exclaimed. "My great-great-grandpappy did a wonderful job on those shelves. The varnish glows!"

"It does," Josie said, looking at the beautiful shelving and counter that William Ferguson had built and delivered...with Jefferson's help. She had paid William with the rest of the money from the loan.

"Speaking of which," she voiced her thoughts aloud, "I have to make money. I've got loan payments to worry about!" A familiar knot in her stomach began, and she breathed in and out.

"You will, Josie. You will."

"Maybe I can't do this, Leigh! What was I thinking? No, I know I can't do this. I can't!"

Josie started pacing, anything to ease the rising anxiety.

"Josie, Josie! You can do this. Please relax. I can't stay long because the baby is up, but you'll be all right. I know it."

"No, I don't think I will be all right. Lock the door! I can't do this. I'll return everything and pay back the loan, and whatever I still owe, I'll work off. I can pick fruit in the Orting valley or whatever I need to do. I could help Will with his fishing business, book clients or whatever!"

Josie moved to the door just as it opened. She jumped back with a shriek, terrified that her first customer was on the point of entering. She wasn't ready. She wasn't ready.

Jefferson popped his head inside.

"Are you open for business?" he said. His smile faded when he saw Josie.

"She's panicking," Leigh said. "Can you calm her down, Jefferson? I have to go. I wish I didn't."

Josie turned to Leigh. "No! You can't leave me! I can't do this alone!"

"I will stay with you, Josie, if you will have me," Jefferson said, stopping Josie from her erratic pacing and taking her hands.

She looked up at him, focusing on his beautiful eyes. "I don't want to do this, Jefferson. I changed my mind."

"Yes, I know that you have. That is fine. You can sell the books and furnishings and repay most of the loan. You could sublease the storefront to someone else."

"I can?" she asked piteously. "You'll show me how to do that?"

"Yes, of course," Jefferson said.

"Oh, Josie," Leigh said in a saddened voice.

Relief flooded through Josie. She breathed in through her nose and clung to Jefferson's fingers, as if drawing strength from him.

"You're right," she said to him, as if no one else existed in the room. "I can do this."

"Wait! What?" Leigh asked, her voice distant.

Josie kept her eyes on Jefferson, who nodded.

"Whatever you want to do," he said.

"I want to own a bookstore," she whispered, tightening her fingers around his.

"And you do." He nodded again.

"I do."

"Wow!" Leigh said. "Okay, I see what's happening here."

Josie thought she should ease her fingers from Jefferson's tight grasp or let him go, but she drew the last bit of strength from him that she could.

"I should let go of you," she said.

"Not until you are ready."

She took one last deep breath and released him. "I'm ready." She blinked and turned to Leigh, almost surprised to see her still standing there.

"You should go," Josie said. "I'll be fine."

"Yes, I can see that," Leigh said. She leaned in to kiss Josie's cheek. "What do you want to do about lunch? You need to eat. Do you want me to bring something over?"

"I will fetch something from the café," Jefferson said. "I will watch over her, Leigh."

"I realize that," she said. "Thank you!" She turned to Josie. "Good luck and many sales!"

She turned to leave, and Josie followed her to the door, suddenly embarrassed by her behavior and Jefferson's rescue. Because that was what he had done. He had rescued her from a panic attack by showing her that she had the freedom to walk away from the project, by releasing her from a feeling of entrapment. He had rescued her by letting her draw strength from his hands, his eyes. The moment had been so intimate that she was bewildered. She was ashamed of the weakness she had shown.

She looked out onto the street, keeping her back to Jefferson yet knowing she should turn around and face him. He came up behind her, and a shiver ran up her back.

"You need a sign over the door," he said.

"I know," she replied, still not turning. "William was making one for me, but he hasn't delivered it yet. I suppose I could stand in the street and announce the bookshop is open for business."

"There is probably no need to do that," Jefferson said. "This is a small town. The word will spread. In fact, here come some ladies now."

Josie froze at the sight of two middle-aged women crossing the street, making a beeline in their direction.

She whirled, fighting another round of rising panic.

"Look at me, Josie. Everything will be all right."

"I know! I know!" She retreated into the store to position herself behind the counter, leaving Jefferson to greet the two women at the door.

"Mrs. Gebhardt, Mrs. Tanner! How nice to see you! Are you coming inside?"

"Mr. Lundrum!" Mrs. Gebhardt exclaimed. "We have come to visit the new bookstore. I cannot tell you how delighted we are to have a bookstore here in Kaskade. We are growing to be so very cosmopolitan!" Gray haired and plump, she seemed very pleasant.

Josie was encouraged by her first customers, and their excitement.

"Mr. Lundrum! Are you the first customer?" said Mrs. Tanner, equally as plump and gray. "We had hoped to be the first! We have been watching the progress of the store."

"I am not the first customer, ladies. You are! May I introduce Miss Josie Brookman, the proprietor?"

He led them to Josie, who thrust out her shaking hand.

"Miss Brookman, allow me to present Mrs. Gebhardt and Mrs. Tanner."

"So delighted to meet you, my dear," Mrs. Tanner said. "Look at those beautiful shelves! I remember this storefront as a junk shop. How very enticing it is now. Very shiny, all glowing!"

"Thank you," Josie said with a wobbly smile. She did her best to breathe deeply. "Mr. William Ferguson from Orting built the shelves and counter. He does wonderful work."

"Indeed he does," Mrs. Gebhardt replied. "I am familiar with his work. Marcy, where are you off to?" she asked Mrs. Tanner. The shorter of the two women had wandered off to a bookshelf.

"I am looking at books, Justine," Mrs. Tanner said. "Is that not why we are here? *I* did not simply come to ogle Miss Brookman!"

"Well, neither did I, Marcy Tanner!"

Mrs. Gebhardt moved over to join Mrs. Tanner in perusing the shelves, and Josie fought back a smile. The ladies were adorable, and she shot Jefferson a wry look.

He leaned across the counter toward her and spoke in a hushed voice. "You could not have hoped for better customers than Mrs. Gebhardt and Mrs. Tanner. Both are very chatty and know everyone in town."

Josie looked up into his eyes, so close to hers. "Thank you," she whispered.

"My pleasure." He straightened and looked around for a chair.

"I don't have anywhere to sit, I'm afraid," Josie said.

"With your permission, I shall bring two from my office. You cannot stand on your feet all day."

"You have my permission," Josie said with a smile.

When it looked as if he was about to go get them, she spoke. "Can you wait until they leave?"

"Certainly!"

An hour passed before Josie felt confident enough to let Jefferson leave. In that time, Mrs. Gebhardt and Mrs. Tanner had bought a book each and other customers had entered the store.

Josie knew she had to let him go, if only for a brief period, and she finally whispered, "I'll be all right. I just need your support this first day. I really appreciate this, Jefferson. I really do!"

"Of course," Jefferson replied.

Thankfully, he returned quite soon with a chair and then went to fetch another. By that time, a steady stream of customers or looky-loos flowed in and out of the store, leaving Josie little time to relax long enough to worry.

Jefferson signaled over a customer's shoulder in the direction of the café, and Josie nodded that she understood. He returned to the store in about half an hour with a basket, which he set behind the counter. As soon as he entered, she knew he had ordered her favorite soup. The smell of fresh bread wafted throughout the shop.

Josie's stomach rumbled in a good way, but she couldn't very well turn her back on the talkative customers and eat. Fifteen minutes after Jefferson returned, he approached Josie while she chatted with an older gentleman.

"Miss Brookman, your lunch is here," he said. "Perhaps I can show this gentleman a few books while you take your lunch break?"

Josie threw him a grateful look. She made her way to the bathroom. Once inside, she leaned on her brand-new antique pedestal sink and stared at her face in the mirror. Her eyes were wide, her cheeks flushed, and she looked not so much anxious as excited. She was excited to own her own store, to be chatting about books, though many of the authors were unfamiliar to her other than she had ordered them. Some were classics, of course, in any century, and they had been easy to select.

She used the facility, washed her hands and left the bathroom. Jefferson, still in conversation with the old gentleman, threw her a quick look as she crossed the room. Josie had the feeling he was worried about her digestive system—a fact that embarrassed her—but she'd had no trouble with her nervous stomach for the past hour. If anything, her excitement had given her an appetite, and she looked forward to some delicious soup.

She picked up the bowl of soup and a slice of bread that Jefferson had thoughtfully laid out, and she settled down in one of his wooden armchairs, hidden by the counter. She ate with relish, listening to the murmurings of Jefferson and the customer. She couldn't hear any specific words, but she trusted Jefferson to either sell a book or entertain the customer so that he'd come back. If anything, Jefferson would excel at the latter. She had already known he had a way with people, and he seemed prepared to deploy those skills in service of the bookstore.

Josie smiled privately. In that moment, she felt happier than she had been in years. She was safe, warm, fed and dressed in beautiful clothing.

She had a bookstore, something she had dreamed of for years but had never had the financial ability to start—not to mention the impossible competition with the corporate mega booksellers.

She was in love, something else she had dreamed of for years but never had the emotional ability to start—not to mention her anxiety drove people crazy and made them run for the hills.

She didn't know how Jefferson felt about her, but he treated her with kindness and patience. That was enough. She felt enough love for both of them. He could be the silent partner in their love affair. That was fine by her.

The door opened, and a familiar male voice spoke, along with that of a familiar female. Josie popped up over the counter.

Will and Martha stood there, a foot between them. Will continued to dress down, wearing overalls he had found at the mercantile. Martha looked far too elegant to be gazing at Will with such adoration.

Kaskade had done its magic. It was clear to see that Will and Martha had fallen in love, as the town seemed to have intended. Further, Josie, the mistake, had fallen in love with a wonderful man. The end of that story was yet to come, or perhaps there was to be no ending. At the moment, Josie did not care. She didn't worry about it. It was enough that Jefferson was her friend.

"Will! Martha!" she called out, setting her food down. "Did you come to buy a book?"

"We came to congratulate you, Josie!" Martha said. "It has been so long since I have seen you. I have only had news of you from Will."

"I'm sorry," Josie said, going around the counter to hug Martha. She looked at Jefferson, who continued perusing books with the customer. "Dealing with the store, ordering books and everything else has taken so much time that I haven't had time to come over."

"And now it seems that you are much busier than before. Are you happy? Everything is so beautiful!"

"I am happy," Josie said. "You look happy yourself."

Martha blushed. "I am well."

Will grinned, his cheeks reddening too.

"Everything looks great, Josie," he said. "Congratulations!"

"Thank you. I know your business is going well because Mrs. Jackson is cooking a lot of fish for dinner."

"I'm enjoying it. It sure beats cutting timber."

"I'll bet," Josie responded. "Not that you would know, of course, because I haven't seen you at the dinner table for a while. I assumed your job was taking a lot of time."

Martha glanced up at Will with rosy cheeks, her angelic face unusually animated and bright. Josie regretted she had been so busy that she missed that they had fallen in love.

"What is my brother doing?" Martha asked, as if changing the subject.

"He's helping me get over my opening-day nerves. I was quite the basket case."

"How kind of him," Martha said. "I cannot stay long, as I have to get back and prepare lunch, but I did want to come see you. Will said he was on his way here and offered to escort me."

"Let me go see what books you have on fishing," Will said with a wink.

"None, actually, Will," Josie said with a chuckle, "but I'll be happy to order some for you."

He laughed and moved over to talk to Jefferson. The older gentleman moved away to study the shelves.

"Martha!" Josie whispered. "What's going on?"

"Where?" Martha looked over her shoulder, as if something had occurred outside.

"Between you and Will. When did this happen? Where has Will been in the evenings?"

"Josie!" Martha exclaimed in a hushed voice. "Nothing happened." Her lips curled. "Oh, all right, yes, something happened. Will came to help me one night with dinner, and he never stopped coming at night. He brings us a lot of fish, *and* he cooks it too. I realized that I simply could not do without him."

"And that's no fish story," Josie murmured, tilting her head to study Will before returning her attention to Martha.

"No, that is definitely not a fish story," she responded with a chuckle.

"Are you getting married?"

Martha's smile trembled. "He has not asked me."

Josie's inclination was to stomp over to Will, tap him on the shoulder and demand that he fulfill his destiny, to seize the opportunity that Kaskade had given him. Will wasn't going to do better in the twenty-first century than he was doing right now. A beautiful, kind woman loved him. No longer would he have to get on the internet to find a date. He could rest assured that no one of Martha's caliber would be lonely enough to search online for a companion like Will had, like Josie had herself.

Besides, he got to work outside. Kaskade had been very, very good to Will.

Perhaps she had stared at Will too long, because Martha whispered, "Please do not say anything to him, Josie. If he wishes to marry me, he will ask."

"I know, Martha. I'll admit I was thinking about it, but he got angry with me the last time I tried to boss him around. He's a big boy. I just hope he makes the right decision. You."

"Oh, Josie," Martha murmured. "Thank you."

Josie hugged Martha, who said she had to leave. Will, apparently keeping one eye on them, turned when Martha pulled away from Josie.

"Are you ready?" he asked Martha, who nodded.

Josie looked at Jefferson, who smiled benevolently at them. Apparently, he realized the two had fallen in love. He would have, Josie supposed, since he probably saw Will there every evening for dinner.

"I can find my own way back, Will, if you wish to stay," Martha said.

"No, I'm coming with you," he said. He looked at Josie and Jefferson. "This is a rare day off, and Martha and I have fish to fry!"

"Fish again," Jefferson said under his breath.

Josie tried not to laugh.

The door opened, and Belinda and Collin entered. The four jostled at the door.

"Belinda! How lovely to see you," Martha said. "I was just leaving. Hello, Collin."

"Hello, Martha. You look wonderful! We have come to see Josie's store."

Josie wasn't as enthusiastic to see Belinda as she might have been. She glanced at Jefferson, who watched Belinda with interest. Tall, beautiful and confident—that might have been what Jefferson liked.

"Will, is it?" Collin said. "I heard you have a fishing guide business. The two of you are very entrepreneurial. I stand in awe."

"Oh yes!" Belinda echoed, moving farther into the store. "This is wonderful. Collin is after me to open an art gallery, and I rather think I might like to. Josie, you will have to teach me how you managed."

Josie's face flushed. "Goodness! I hardly know myself. Jefferson helped me. Leigh helped me. Mr. Ferguson from Orting helped me. So many people."

"Josie is too modest," Jefferson said, throwing Josie a look she could only describe as proud. "None of us has her knowledge and experience with books. She was a librarian, you know."

Martha threw Josie a smile. "That is no fish story."

"I beg your pardon?" Belinda asked.

Josie would have winked at Martha if she could wink. She settled for a grin.

CHAPTER SEVENTEEN

Jefferson stepped into his office, hung up his jacket and hat and moved over to the window. As he had done every morning for the past month, he opened the window and looked down on Josie's store—*their* store, for William Ferguson had carved and hung the store sign: *Josie Jefferson Bookstore.*

William had forgotten to carve the word "and" between Josie and Jefferson, and they had mutually agreed that the sign would do. Jefferson had been flattered to see his name included, though in truth he was much more touched to see it snugged up next to Josie's name.

He very much wanted to see her name next to his in perpetuity. Jefferson and Josie Lundrum. Still, he dared not ask. Josie was happy with the store. She had been doing well, requiring very little in the way of assistance. He had taken to eating lunch with her every day, and in that way he was able to provide her a break. Martha prepared a small picnic lunch for them, and Jefferson carried it over to the store around noon, where he and Josie ate together.

As if that were not enough, Jefferson had begun stopping by the store every morning to greet Josie, where she presented him with one of Mrs. Jackson's delicious pastries she had brought from the house.

All in all, things were going swimmingly for Josie, and Jefferson did not wish to disrupt the calm, happy ambience by offering marriage and forcing Josie to make a decision on staying or leaving the following year.

He was going to ask her to marry him, of that there was no doubt, but he suspected the timing was critical. Certainly he must ask her before the next summer solstice.

He turned from the window and settled down at his desk. Will had proposed to Martha. The progression of their romance had been clear, concise and inevitable. Kaskade had chosen them for each other, and although at first glance they had seemed opposites, they had found love. Martha, the indoor homemaker, made time to go out fishing on the lake with her beloved, and Will, the outdoorsman, made time to go into the kitchen with Martha. They had formed a partnership, as had he and Josie.

However, neither Martha nor Will had Josie's anxious nature. Though Josie's worries seemed to have calmed a great deal in the past month, she was still prone to occasional fretting. Jefferson accepted that she always would be, and he loved her—not despite her nature but because of it. To him, an excess of worrying meant an excess of caring. Had Josie not cared about things, she would not have worried.

He returned to the window. As if on cue, Josie opened the door and stepped outside to look up at him. He waved, and she waved back. His heart swelled. What man did not wish to see the woman he loved thriving and happy to see him.

Mrs. Gebhardt and Mrs. Tanner approached the store, and Josie gave him one last wave as she greeted the ladies. The door closed behind them, and he settled back down at his desk.

Jefferson worked steadily for an hour until a strange smell caught his attention. Coming from outside the window, the odor smelled strangely like wood burning. Hardly a common smell in the middle of summer when temperatures were warm and fireplaces cold, he rose to look out the window.

His eyes naturally gravitated toward Josie's store, where the door was shut. He willed Josie to open the door and wave at him, but she did not. Something odd caught his eyes.

There, beneath the door, a band of white formed, as if flowing out under the door.

Smoke! Fire!

Jefferson yelled out the window. "Fire! Josie! Josie!"

The door did not open, although several people in the street turned to look at him. He saw Mrs. Gebhardt and Mrs. Tanner near the mercantile. They were not in the bookstore then.

Jefferson ran down the stairs, shouting. Sprinting across the street, he panicked as the smell of smoke grew stronger. Smoke billowed out from under Josie's door.

Bells sounded nearby, the town's emergency fire alarm. People started running toward the store. Out of the corner of Jefferson's eye, he saw men lining up at a nearby horse trough with buckets of water.

He wrenched open the door, and a thick wall of smoke hit him like a solid object. Dropping down to his knees to see better, he shouted for Josie.

"Josie! Josie!"

There was no answer. A wall of heat assailed him as flames made themselves known.

"Take this!" a man yelled from the street as he threw a wet jacket toward Jefferson. Jefferson wrapped it over his head and crawled into the store, calling Josie's name over and over.

His voice was drowned out by the din of shouting outside as men lined up to throw buckets of water into the store. For a moment, Jefferson mourned the loss of Josie's work, as her books would either burn or suffer water damage, but the thought was fleeting. His priority was finding Josie. He prayed that she was not in the bathroom at the rear of the store, for the flames made reaching the back impossible.

"Josie!" he kept shouting. He slithered about on the floor, trying to feel for her. He bumped into the counter, not yet on fire, and turned to the right toward the center. The crackle of the flames and shouts of men throwing water into the store continued to drown out his voice.

"Josie!" he yelled. He felt one booted foot and then another, albeit motionless. He scrambled to his knees, shouldering the jacket that covered his head. He grabbed Josie's feet and pulled her toward him, away from the flames. His lungs burned from smoke and heat as he struggled for air.

Josie's arms were full of books, and Jefferson realized she must have been trying to save some of the books when she succumbed to the smoke. He pushed the books aside and pulled her into his arms. Rising to a standing position with effort, he worked his way back to the entrance by following the shouting. Twice he was pelted with a bucket of water before he shouted at the would-be firemen to let him through.

He made it outside with Josie and stepped off the boardwalk, uncertain how much of the building was burning. His eyes stung, and his breathing was labored. He reached the opposite side of the street, when a man came running toward him. Jefferson staggered and fell to his knees under Josie's weight and his own weakness.

Jeremiah threw himself down at their side, checking Josie for a pulse.

"Is she alive?" Jefferson asked hoarsely. "Please say that she is alive."

Jeremiah nodded. "She is alive."

Over Jeremiah's shoulder, Jefferson saw Leigh run up to them, Martha and Will on her heels. The smoke rising up from the store would have caught the attention of many townspeople. Men worked to dampen the connecting building and the mercantile—successfully, it would seem, as the flames appeared to be dying down.

"Her breathing is labored. We need to get her home and away from the smoke," Jeremiah said. "Let me see about getting a wagon."

"Is she all right?" Leigh cried out.

"Yes, I believe so," Jeremiah said.

Martha and Will reached his side.

Jefferson looked at the chaos in the street. A wagon could not get through the melee of people helping to put out the fire.

"No wagon will get through here. I will carry her."

"Jefferson, you are in no shape to do that," Jeremiah barked. "Look at your hands! I need to attend to you as well."

Jefferson looked down at his hands, red angry blisters already rising from burns he had acquired in the store. In terror, he looked down at Josie and pushed aside the hair from her face. Other than streaks of gray ash, her skin looked unharmed.

"She is not burnt," Jeremiah said.

"Thank goodness! I will carry her," Jefferson said.

"Oh, Jefferson," Martha cooed. "How can you?"

"I'll help carry her," Will said.

"Will and I will form a chair and carry her," Jeremiah said.

"No, I will help," Jefferson insisted, adamant.

"Very well. We should not quibble. Slide your hands under her. Will, grasp his arms. Take care that you do not grab his hands, as they are burned."

"Oh man! Those look painful!" Will said, looking down at Jefferson's hands.

"Do not worry about me. They will mend. Are you ready?"

Will nodded. Together they scooped Josie up and carried her down the road away from the smoke. Jeremiah, Leigh and Martha followed.

"The fire is out!" Jefferson heard several voices shouting from behind them. He looked over his shoulder to see smoke continuing to waft from the open door and men holding empty buckets, congratulating one another. He stumbled and turned his attention to his footing. The back of his hands stung, but he would not have let go for the world.

"Will she be all right, Jeremiah?" he asked hoarsely as he and Will balanced Josie. His throat hurt both from shouting and the smoke, and he found it difficult to talk.

"I hope so," Jeremiah said. "If she regains consciousness, I must assess damage to her lungs."

"*If* she regains consciousness?" Jefferson repeated.

"I can make no guarantees, Jefferson."

Jefferson looked down at Josie's face lolling in the crook of his shoulder. "Josie, wake up, please," he whispered. "Josie."

She did not awaken, however. They reached the house in what seemed like an interminable time, and they carried Josie into Jeremiah's examining room, depositing her on the examination table.

"I think I have done this before," Jeremiah said. "Poor girl."

Will went to join Martha at the doorway as Jeremiah set about examining Josie.

"Perhaps you should step outside and close the door, Jefferson. I want to remove this smoke-laden clothing. Martha, could you assist me?"

Jefferson left the office reluctantly and waited in the parlor. Leigh brought a tray of lemonade in and requested that Jefferson and Will both drink some. The liquid was delightful on Jefferson's sore throat. Will and Martha sat down, but Jefferson opted to stand.

"My clothing is smoke laden. I do not wish to ruin your furniture."

Leigh did not argue.

"I wish I could go in there and help, but Jeremiah knows I struggle with his examination room," she said.

"I remember," Jefferson said. "Your mother was ill for a long time, and you suffered through many doctors during her illness."

"Yes," Leigh said simply.

"Will she be all right, Leigh?" Jefferson could not help but ask again. "You know more about modern medicine that we do. Will she be all right with what Jeremiah has available to him in 1910?"

Leigh shook her head "I don't know, Jefferson. I really don't know."

"She'll be all right, Jefferson," Will said. "I know she will."

Jefferson looked at Will. "How do you know? Have you seen this before? What complications could arise? Will she awaken?"

Jefferson couldn't hold back his questions.

"I'm no expert, but I'm sure she'll wake up. She was breathing, and her color wasn't bad. She wasn't blue. The only thing I think Jeremiah would worry about now is the damage from smoke inhalation. He won't know anything until she awakens."

"She shouldn't be here," Jefferson muttered. "She was a mistake. She shouldn't be here."

"Jefferson," Leigh murmured. "I know you're upset, but she's not a mistake."

He looked up from staring at the carpet. "I do not mean her existence is a mistake, Leigh, only that she was not meant to travel back in time, was she?"

"I hate to disagree with you when you're upset, man, but I disagree," Will said. "Her time travel was no mistake, no matter what she says. She was meant to be here. She's changed a lot since she's been here. She's happier than she was."

"But not safer," Jefferson growled, turning toward the examining room door to listen for her voice.

"Since you haven't lived in my time, I don't know how you can say that. Believe me, she's safer here...with you."

"It's true, Jefferson," Leigh said. "She loves you. She was meant to come here."

Jefferson turned back to them. "Love!" His voice was bitter. "What good has that done her? I love her, but I could not protect her!"

"Jefferson, you're just upset," Leigh said, coming to his side and taking his arm. "You'll feel better when you get to see her."

Jefferson gritted his teeth and tried to calm down. If the anxiety he felt now was anything like what Josie had suffered, he sympathized greatly. His head ached and his stomach churned. His hands burned and his throat hurt, but he recalled those were due to the fire.

"I do not even know how the fire started. Poor Josie. She worked so hard on the store. She did not deserve this."

"No, she didn't. I'm sure she'll tell us when she wakes up. She can rebuild."

Jefferson found himself oddly irritated by Leigh's comfort. He was worried, and the worry kept him from grief. He wanted to fret.

"Yes, of course" was all that he said. He moved away from Leigh and positioned himself closer to the door.

"How long must we wait?" he muttered at the door.

As if she heard him, Martha opened the door. She enveloped her brother in a rare hug, and Jefferson's heart broke. Josie had died. There was no other reason for Martha to embrace him. None.

He disentangled herself and pushed her from him.

"No!" he ground out in a strangled voice. "No!"

Will jumped up to come to Martha's side.

"Jefferson!" Martha protested.

"No, she is not dead! I will not have it. I will not! Do not speak those words!"

Jefferson pushed open the examining room door and stormed into the room. There on the examining table sat Josie, upright and alive, beautiful in her disheveled state.

"Jefferson!" Jeremiah protested as Jefferson crossed the room and wrapped his arms around Josie. "Let loose of her now. She must breathe."

Jefferson heard Jeremiah's words and released Josie. She tried to talk, but nothing came from her open mouth. She reached a hand to her throat.

"Forgive me. I thought the worst," Jefferson said.

"No need to think the worst," Jeremiah said. "We need to watch

Josie to ensure she does not contract pneumonia, but she will recover her voice. However, ardent embracing is out of the question for now."

Jefferson's face reddened, and he turned and looked over his shoulder at the three faces watching from the doorway.

"Forgive me," he said to all three. "My anxiety was uncontrollable."

He returned his attention to Josie and took her hands.

"I love you, Josie. I love you."

Her mouth worked, and tears ran down her eyes. She nodded her head and lifted one of his hands to her mouth. Her eyes widened at the blisters on the hand, and she shook her head and held it up as if to get Jeremiah's attention.

"Yes, I know. Next!" Jeremiah called out.

Chapter Eighteen

A week later, Josie waited on the porch for Jefferson, who had an appointment with Jeremiah to get his bandages changed. She had developed pneumonia from the inhalation, for which Jeremiah had prescribed movement, particularly walking. Jefferson had come to walk with her every day.

Josie had waited for Jefferson to tell her that he loved her again, but he hadn't. She didn't know what to expect or what he wanted from those words. Maybe he'd just said them in the heat of the moment.

She hadn't returned to the store yet, Jeremiah preferring that she stay clear of smoke residue, dust or ashes. Jefferson had hired some men to clear out the store. Through his eyes, she had seen the shelves bare of books. Those that had not burned had been damaged by water. The shelves themselves remained standing, and William Ferguson had come down to sand them and revarnish them. Jefferson had gone further and had the walls and floors sanded and revarnished.

"You will start over when you are well," he told her.

They had speculated on how the fire started. Josie reported that a customer had entered with a cigar, and she had asked the man to extinguish it outside. He had gone outside to do so. Josie recalled that he had left the door open, and she saw him stubbing the cigar out on the boardwalk. She thought no more about it when he reentered. Sometime later, the fire started, and she speculated that a burning ash had blown in the open door and caught one of the books.

"I wished I'd seen the fire brigade," she said when Jefferson described how the fire was extinguished. "Are they regular firemen or volunteers?"

"No, the townspeople just come together in those situations. Fires are not uncommon," he said, "and people know how to rally in those events."

Josie wondered about finances.

"I can't afford another loan, Jefferson. I don't know how I'm going to pay this one back."

"You could add another ten cents to each book and continue your payments and the purchase of new books."

"Oh! I guess I could. I never thought of that. I'm more librarian than I am businesswoman, I guess."

Jefferson smiled. "I will admit that I asked for advice at the mercantile. They had a small fire some years ago, and I wondered how they managed. They added a small percentage to each item sold."

"Did the store sign survive?" Josie asked.

"It did," he assured her.

"I'm so glad."

"As am I."

Josie waited again to see if he would repeat his words of love, but he didn't. She didn't have the heart to prod him. She had come a long way in the last few months. In the past, she couldn't have contained her anxiety and would have worried incessantly about his feelings, about the future of the store, about her health, about his hands. But she felt relatively calm at the moment as she waited for Jefferson with an almost que será, será attitude. If she had learned nothing over the past few months, it was that she couldn't change anything, she couldn't force anything and she couldn't make anything happen that wasn't meant to happen.

Finally, Jefferson entered the gate and walked up to the porch. He sat down beside Josie.

"Belinda and Collin send their best wishes," Jefferson said.

"Oh, you've seen them?"

"Yes, Collin works across the hall from me."

"That's right."

"What was that in your tone?"

"Tone?" Josie stalled.

"Yes, Josie, your tone."

Josie took a deep breath. She couldn't change anything.

"Are you interested in Belinda?"

"Interested in Belinda?" Jefferson repeated.

"You don't have to repeat it. Just tell me."

"I have known Belinda for many years. I may even have liked her very much when we were younger, but I like someone else very much now. Truthfully, I am glad to be able to confide in you, Josie. You see, I am very much in love. I love this little tawny-haired woman to distraction. The sight of her makes my stomach churn, my head ache, my heart swell and my knees shake. The sound of her voice calms my fears and soothes that same head ache. The touch of her hand on my arm makes me feel as if I am on top of the world...and she beside me."

Josie felt like she was drowning in his words.

"She makes me nervous and she makes me happy. She delights me and frightens me. She makes me ill and she makes me well. But above all, she makes me love her. I cannot help myself, and I do not wish to. What I would truly like is to spend the rest of my days with her. Josie Jefferson Emporium."

With the tips of the fingers poking out from his bandages, he wiped away the tears from her face.

"Would you like to be my partner, Josie? Silent, vocal, business, romantic, beloved and forever? Will you marry me?"

"I thought I was a mistake," she whispered.

"You were never a mistake to me."

"What about the way I am? Doesn't that drive you crazy?"

Jefferson nodded. "It does indeed. You drive me crazy, and I love it! I love you. What about the way I am? Does that drive you crazy?"

"You're perfect, Jefferson. You're just perfect for me."

"As you are to me, my love. Perfection in every way. Did you say that you would marry me?"

"Silently," Josie said with a grin. "Silently."

About the Author

Bess McBride is the best-selling author of over twenty time travel romances as well as contemporary, historical, romantic suspense and light paranormal romances. She loves to hear from readers, and you can contact her at bessmcbride@gmail.com. She also writes short cozy mysteries as Minnie Crockwell. You can visit her website at www.bessmcbride.com.

www.ingramcontent.com/pod-product-compliance
Lightning Source LLC
Chambersburg PA
CBHW050525160726
48003CB00001B/457